# Baby and the Billionaire

Victoria Sue

# Chapter One

Zeke wasn't sure how long he'd been lying in his own piss, sweat, and blood. He couldn't say if it had been days or weeks. Pain seemed to blend them seamlessly into one another. With a detached air, he registered the door opening again. He knew the questions would start soon, then pain would follow when they didn't get the answers they wanted. Although the longer the questions went on, the more confused he was getting about what the right answer *was*. He'd started out defiant. Trina was a child and her mother, Elena, was cruel. Marco was Trina's brother. He trusted Marco and wanted to help. He didn't trust their mother, Elena, the Panthera of the West Coast, so when he'd been asked to help hide Trina, of course he had.

Bit by bit, that had changed though. The people asking him questions minute after minute, hour after hour, differed, until the same man started appearing. Could he at least admit he wasn't a fan of the panther clan system?

The utter relief of being able to answer a question with a "yes" made him almost giddy with relief. He'd wanted to cry at being able to agree, and he'd been rewarded for it. For the first time he'd been helped to get clean and had his injuries treated. When the questions had started again, they seemed less aggressive, persuasive almost. He had suffered so much under the panther clan system. His beautiful lover—Emmett's mom—the woman he had wanted to spend his life with had been killed because of it. Surely that was wrong, wouldn't he agree? And, of course, he did. He seemed to agree with quite a lot of what he said. He wasn't foolish and he knew he would have agreed to almost anything to stop the beatings, but he was only saying what Zeke felt. It was no hardship to agree that what they had done to Josie was murderous. It was no struggle to agree that if Trina was brought up by the same woman who had killed Josie that the whole cycle would start again. What would happen to the next panther female who fell in love with a human male? Would she be killed as well?

He'd managed once to question the system. How was this Panthera—Elena—any different to Emmett's grandma, Regina? Marco hadn't seemed to think so. Then the man had smiled and had brought out evidence to show Zeke that Elena had known where Marco had been for years, but more importantly, she had left him alone. Whereas Josie—under Regina's watch—had been murdered.

He'd protested again saying that Regina hadn't known. That Josie's brother had worked independently, and that Regina was innocent. But the man had thought the idea was amusing, that a Panthera used to the same sort of power and control that Elena had would have been so easily duped. And he pointed out the proof of how easily Elena had found Marco. That surely Zeke didn't think that Regina hadn't had exactly the same access to information. Information—he should know—was readily available to those with money to purchase it.

And doubt had crept in. Day after day, hour after hour, until Zeke really wasn't sure of anything anymore.

Then they dropped the final bombshell: that if Trina wasn't "rescued" from the murderess and returned to her mother, the East and West coast clans would be at war. After all, wouldn't Zeke risk everything he had to protect his own son and granddaughter? He could hardly blame Elena for feeling the same way. And when the war came, Josie—who had been named after the dead woman he had adored who had been killed under Regina's watch, he was reminded —and his pack would be in the middle, and if there was a war, there would be nothing Elena could do to protect the innocent.

But what was he supposed to do? How could he get to Trina—if he *agreed* of course, because he wasn't sure he did. The man nodded sympathetically and said he understood, that he was sorry. It was clear Zeke was an honorable man and he apologized for his treatment because they had mistakenly thought he supported a young girl being kidnapped and forced away from the family that adored her. In fact, now they realized they owed him a debt. He had kept Trina safe for the last few months and Elena owed him for it. When the war came, they would do their best to keep Emmett and Josie away from harm. Their *best*, but they couldn't guarantee it.

"What do you need me to do to make that happen? To make sure Emmett and Josie are safe?"

The words were out before Zeke had even known he was going to say them, and shame silenced him.

The man nodded his head. He understood loyalty and knew that Zeke's first loyalty was to his son and granddaughter. Again he promised they would do their best to keep Emmett and Josie safe. A shame he was mated to the alpha and would be unlikely to leave him.

Of course, Emmett wouldn't leave Ryker. The man stood up and said he would have a car brought around and did Zeke want the be taken back to the pack house or his offices in Asheville? Zeke's first thought was to go and lick his wounds in private like he had always done. But maybe he needed to address the problem head on.

"The Blue Ridge pack," he whispered from cracked dried lips.

Three hours later, he was there.


Ryker sat and listened to the old man's son. Somehow—apparently— they had robbed his father of the land he owned to the west of their property. Ryker knew Zeke had purchased the land legally. He had given the man exactly the price he had asked for, but now the old man had died, and his sons didn't seem to agree with the deal that had been struck. Apparently, it had been theft, even though Zeke had paid slightly over comparable property values. Never mind that neither of the two sons had been in their father's life recently, otherwise they could have advised him at the time. Supposedly the old man had been "difficult", which was soon changed to "senile." They'd added Alzheimer's for good measure, much to Ryker's disgust, as if it was some buzz word and not a heartbreaking illness a lot of humans suffered from. The last time Zeke had met Jeb Davies the man had been delighted to sell his land. He'd cackled and said he had altered his will and cut out both of his no-good sons. Instead, he would be donating half his estate to a breast cancer charity to help fight the same disease that had killed his wife, and the rest was going to a neighbor who had acted more like family to him than his own.

"Pops wouldn't like some hippy commune shit setting up here." Ryker didn't respond and kept his temper in check. Paxton Davies disgusted him. Not just because he didn't seem to be too fond of personal cleanliness, or because he thought being armed with a handgun strapped to a belt that barely made it around his huge beer belly might intimidate Ryker. No, it was the way he clearly expected a bullying attitude was going to work. He had gotten too up close and personal with Ryker almost immediately, and despite the smell, Ryker neither stepped back nor reacted. After a brief standoff, Paxton used the excuse of ordering a third, younger man out of the truck to step away from Ryker.

Ryker took a moment to focus on Paxton's brother. Porter, who seemed close in age to Paxton, was physically very different. He was whipcord thin, covered in what looked like self-inflicted tattoos—possibly prison issue—and stank of smoke. He didn't have a handgun though. He stood casually, leaning on the back of their pickup and balancing a hunting rifle across his folded arms.

Ryker dismissed him as his attention was caught by the young

4

man who scrambled from the truck and ran right up to Paxton with an envelope. Then he froze and instead of handing the envelope to Paxton he slowly brought his head around to stare at Ryker.

He was...*battered* was the only word Ryker could come up with. If he was twenty years old Ryker would have been surprised. But what caught Ryker's attention were the myriad bruises on his arms, the split lip, and the fading yellow bruise on his cheek.

"No," he whispered and seemed to shrink into himself. Ryker took a concerned step forward and the man shrank back to Paxton.

*What the fuck?* He was scared of *him*? When he was with two bullying assholes who were clearly responsible for the beatings?

Then he caught it, a faint, barely there scent of shifter. *But not which.*

"Get your fat ass back in the truck, Bobby." Porter ordered, but the boy didn't move.

He heard a faint growl from Red, but Ryker knew neither human would have. It seemed to be the last straw for the young man though. The envelope slipped from his shaking fingers, and he turned blindly. Ryker knew he was going to run, but Porter, who had obviously lost his patience, took hold of Bobby's arm and shoved him in the truck. Bobby made no attempt to get back out, he just curled up in the corner.

"I got the details of my lawyer here." Paxton said gruffly like there was nothing wrong, then picked up the envelope from the ground and shoved it at Ryker. "We'll be in touch."

But Ryker was barely listening. Every one of his alpha senses was screaming in confusion because he couldn't identify Bobby's shifter scent. The boy reeked of stale smoke, but that shouldn't mask his smell. Ryker didn't look behind him. He could still hear the faint rumble from Red's wolf and knew the man had seen the bruises.

Porter spat noisily on the ground, then both brothers returned to their pickup and drove away.

Ryker pulled out the paper and scanned the bad attempt at legal intimidation which mentioned hunting rights along with a shit ton of other stuff that Zeke would know how to deal with.

*Zeke.* Ryker sighed gustily. It had been ten days. Emmett was distraught. Darriel was turning into a ghost before their very eyes. And Ryker had been fucking useless. They'd been combing the surrounding countryside, but they had gotten nowhere. Even Regina hadn't been able to get any information.

It was as if Zeke had just vanished like smoke.

He glanced at Red, who he'd expected to have an immediate opinion on the brothers, but Red was still staring down the road even though the pickup had disappeared. The man was *furious.* Jaw tense, he stood almost frozen, brown eyes glittering dangerously. "Red."

Red seemed to drag his gaze from the empty road with difficulty and he took a breath. "I don't like bullies."

Neither did Ryker, but with Shifter Rescue and doing what they did, this wasn't the first time they'd seen someone in the shape Bobby was in and he'd never seen Red react like this. "I'm going to call May. Find out how exactly who he is and his age, and we'll take it from there."

Red nodded and they turned to the truck. "And he wasn't fat," Red mumbled. "Just human soft."

It was a good thing Red was walking in front of him and didn't see Ryker's jaw nearly hit the floor. *Human soft?* Red hadn't smelled shifter? But before he could comment, he felt his cell phone vibrate with a notification. He ignored it. He'd agreed to meet the Davies brothers at the edge of their father's old land. There was no way—even though they'd asked—he could allow them on pack territory. There were too many kids now and the possibility for unexpected first shifts was high. He wanted to make sure that all the pups, cubs, whatever, were safe.

*Not just mine.* He allowed himself a small smile as he got in the jeep.

"You think they're gonna be trouble?"

Ryker glanced at Red. They'd been friends for a long damn time.

He'd been one of Ryker's greatest supporters, even though he could easily be an alpha himself. "They're dumb, but they might have not so-dumb lawyers."

Ryker nearly commented on the boy's scent, but something told him to keep quiet, which was doubly strange because he shared almost everything with Red.

"And the trouble is the one person you'd get to handle this isn't here."

Ryker nodded, unable to speak for a moment. "Do we have an update from Regina?"

Red huffed. "To be honest, I've never seen her genuinely angry before. She's furious, but it's like it's contained. If you'd have asked me any time up to Riggs involving Emmett, I would have said it was because of pride. That she hated anyone or anything getting one over on her. But now? Not so much." He put the truck into drive. "The most unlikely woman in the entire universe loves being a grandma."

Ryker smiled. In any other circumstances he would have laughed, but his sense of humor had disappeared along with Zeke. Emmett was beside himself, but it was Darriel who was really worrying him. He'd been there for his twins, of course. Emmeline and Karina were thriving. But Darriel seemed to grow more distant every day. He was barely eating, and Ryker genuinely believed if it wasn't for the girls, he'd be really sick.

Ryker's cell phone buzzed again, and he fished it out of his back pocket. It was TJ, one of his betas managing security for the compound today. "Ryker," the man rushed out in a stunned voice. "I'm at the bottom gate and I have Zeke."

"Fuck," Ryker swore. "How is he?"

"He wants you to come down here for him." Red could obviously hear because he turned the truck around and headed down the hill.

"Is he okay? Does he need a doctor?"

"He's standing," TJ said bluntly and hung up.

Ryker looked at Red who was gazing grimly at the road. Ryker's finger hovered over the button to call the pack house.

"I wouldn't yet," Red said.

"You don't think—"

"TJ said he was standing, not that he was okay. Another few minutes for us to get there and see him for ourselves won't make any difference."

"Maybe I should call Marco?" At the very least. He was their medic.

"Zeke has enough money to get a doctor if he wants one."

Ryker nodded. "You're right. I just wanted to tell Emmett."

Red shot him an understanding look. "Let's just wait until you've seen him." For all Red was trying to caution patience, he drove down the road like he had a lead foot.

Ryker's eyes immediately landed on his friend. Zeke stood talking to TJ and two of the gammas. He was out of the truck and running before Red had brought it to a proper stop. He took in the bruises and swelling in Zeke's face, the sunken cheeks and the stiff way he was standing.

"What the fuck are you doing down here. You need—"

But Zeke put his shaky hand up. "Walk with me." He turned and limped away from the group, Ryker following him. He stopped when he was confident the shifters wouldn't be able to hear. "We have a problem."

Ryker almost scoffed, but the look in his friend's blood-shot eyes silenced him.

"I've just been subjected to a very clever persuasive attack."

"Persuasive?" Ryker echoed and something more than simple fear for his friend coiled in his belly. "What does that mean?"

"They knew what they were doing. By the time they'd finished I had agreed to help them get Trina away from the monster that killed Josie."

Ryker inhaled sharply knowing Zeke had never gotten over his lover's death. He remembered how the normally tough guy had nearly cried when Emmett said they were naming their baby Josie after her.

"There's a clan war about to happen and Emmett and Josie will be stuck in the middle of it unless I tell them how to get to Trina."

"You—" But Ryker cut off the words. If Zeke was going to do it, he wouldn't be standing here warning Ryker.

"If it's true and they are going to start a clan war—if such a thing even exists?"

Ryker shook his head. *A clan war?* He doubted it. Panther clans were too civilized, for want of a better word. Not that the claw—the panther version of wolf enforcers—wouldn't kill or torture at the order of the Panthera, but he couldn't see anything happening that would risk outside attention. "How can a "war" be hidden from the humans?"

"I have no idea," Zeke admitted, "but I intend to find out."

Ryker firmly pressed his lips together again. Zeke was clever but was still human. He was pretty sure most of the adolescents in the pack could best him strength-wise in a physical fight. "Assuming that is the right thing to do, and we need to have a real long talk about it first, how the fuck are you going to manage it?"

Zeke smiled, then hissed as his face clearly hurt. "I'm going to let Elena think I'm on board."

Ryker huffed. "We need to tell Regina."

"Absolutely not," Zeke snapped out. "Elena gets one whiff of this and you're putting Emmett and Josie in the firing line. We need to be the only people who know for the time being."

"I don't like it."

Zeke nodded and put his hand on Ryker's shoulder. "You think I do?"

Ryker gazed at his friend then shook his head.

"Good." But Zeke didn't let go. "Then for pity's sake, get me back to the pack house so Marco can give me shifter-strength painkillers. We'll talk later, but this stays between me and you."

Ryker walked back to the truck, aware that Zeke was using him to keep upright. He wasn't happy agreeing not to involve Regina, but he would see what else Zeke had to say first. Ryker eyed his friend. He trusted Zeke, he really did, but Josie had died on Regina's watch, and he knew Zeke had never forgiven the Panthera for it.

If he was Zeke, he wasn't sure how much persuading it might take to pursue revenge, especially if Zeke thought he was saving Emmett and Josie in the process. He wasn't sure at all.

# Chapter Two

They were two steps from the pack house when Zeke heard the shout and looked up as Emmett came flying toward him. "Dad!"

Ryker moved quickly to intercept his mate. "Careful. He's sore."

Emmett took one horrified look at him and his face crumpled. Dinah and Chrissy hurried out along with a few more of the pack. Zeke opened his arms and smiled at his son even though it cost him. He'd been feeling increasingly weird and shaky as they drove. Emmett gently embraced him. "Dad."

Zeke closed his eyes in relief and hugged Emmett tightly despite his bruised body protesting. There had been a lot of black moments during his captivity when he doubted he would get to see his son again. "You're hot," Emmett said in a worried tone.

"Let's get you inside." Zeke looked up and saw Marco. He nodded, exhaustion snapping at him. Adrenaline had gotten him here when he realized the clan was letting him go, but it was waning quickly. The pack house suddenly seemed a very long way away.

"Okay everyone. Let's give him some space," Ryker ordered and came closer to Zeke. Marco appeared on his other side. Zeke concentrated on putting one foot in front of the other, and with little fuss Ryker managed to get him to the clinic and up on the exam table. Emmett pulled out a stool and refused to let go of his hand, not that he was complaining. The room seemed to be going in and out of focus though.

"How did you escape?" Emmett asked.

Zeke met Ryker's eyes knowing he would understand why he had to lie. "I never saw anyone I recognized," he explained. "Things were rough for quite a while." He quieted while Marco gently opened his shirt buttons. He saw the shock on Emmett's face and imagined the rest. "Then one day someone different arrived, he patched me up, cleaned and fed me, and dropped me back here. They wanted to know where Trina was. When I said I didn't know, they gave up asking." Which was a very rough—

The door to the clinic slammed open and Darriel stood there heaving a breath. He gazed at Zeke, put a shaky hand to his mouth, then turned and fled. Zeke closed his eyes to stop them smarting. Then he opened them to complete and utter silence. Zeke glanced helplessly at Marco. Marco was the only one to whom he'd admitted how he felt about Darriel. Or not exactly, because no matter how he felt he was still too damn old. Emmett stood. "Are you hungry, Dad?"

Zeke smiled wanly. "Not really."

"You look beat," Ryker said, joining Emmett in changing the subject or at least glossing over what had just happened. He hissed as Marco touched his ribs, nausea rolling over him. He gritted his teeth and Ryker read his expression. He asked Emmett to help him make sure the room Zeke slept in when he visited was ready. Zeke loved Emmett but right then he could have kissed Ryker for guiding him away.

"Not broken, but without an X-ray I can't be a hundred percent certain. Let's look at your back. Can you lean forward?"

"Do I have to?" Zeke tried to joke. The pain in his back hurt more than his black eye or ribs.

Marco helped him gently ease forward. He took in the hastily applied dressings that had been hidden under his shirt, then inch by excruciating inch removed them. Zeke was lightheaded by the time he was done. He tried to focus on Marco with difficulty, really glad he was sitting down. Marco was silent for a moment as he regarded his back. Zeke knew it was bad.

"They whipped you." It was a statement of fact. Zeke knew he didn't have to confirm it. "And they're badly infected." Marco came to stand in front of Zeke so he didn't have to twist his neck to look at him. "You have a fever, but you also have choices. I'm not a doctor, but in my opinion because you're a human, not just a non-shifter, you should be in the hospital." He heard the door open as Marco said that and recognized Ryker, although he was a little fuzzy around the edges. Ryker stepped forward, listening to Marco. Marco shot Ryker a worried glance.

"Antibiotics? Do we need to call the chopper? I can get May—"

"No." Zeke gritted his teeth and fixed his gaze on Ryker as much as he could. "You know I can't let the humans see this. They'd involve the cops." It was getting hard to concentrate. "If you tell May what you need, she'll get it."

Marco looked at Ryker as if for permission.

"My body, Ryker. You can't pull your alpha crap with me." Which, if he had been conscious enough to think about, would have been quite funny.

Everything was very fuzzy after that. His back hurt like a mother-fucker and he felt like his body was literally boiling from the inside out. Everything hurt. Even in the moments when he knew he was lying in a bed somewhere and someone was holding his hand. After a while the hand started to feel a little familiar. Long, slim fingers took his so reassuringly. Sometimes they held something cool to his face. Sometimes glorious ice chips were pushed between cracked lips and just allowed to melt. Then the same hand would carefully smooth something on his lips to stop them from hurting.

Zeke wished...but he didn't know what for. He ached to be able to force his heavy eyes open and see the face that belonged to the hand. He knew who it was somehow, even though he couldn't remember a name. Then, on the fifth day—not that he knew that until afterwards—he cracked open his eyes and the room came into focus. His gaze immediately dropped to the delicate fingers holding his and the figure resting his head on his other folded arm.

Darriel was asleep. Zeke greedily drank him in, from the bruised black shadows under each closed eye to the hollowed-out cheeks, even more so than before, to the hand holding onto his as though he were a life raft. He was more likely to make Darriel drown, but selfishly he didn't seem to be able to let go. He sensed movement beside him and turned to see Marco holding a glass of water and angling a straw to his lips. It was heavenly.

Marco nodded to the bed and Zeke returned his gaze to the sleeping young man, except now he wasn't. Deep brown eyes gazed at him, reflecting a million worries and as many doubts. "I need to go get some more dextrose for you." Zeke followed Marco's gaze to the IV bag hanging on a pole beside the bed and draining into his vein. Marco shut the door behind him.

Hesitantly, Darriel reached out with his other hand and lightly tucked some of Zeke's normally short hair behind his ears. Zeke almost moaned at the touch he'd wanted for so long. He should tell him to go, but he couldn't form the words. He had no defenses around this beautiful man.

"Do you want me to go?" Darriel whispered as if he had plucked that thought right out of Zeke's brain.

Zeke's fingers tightened on Darriel's reflexively. God help him, but no, he didn't want Darriel to go. "What about the girls?"

Darriel nodded to the corner where the twin stroller stood. Zeke felt his eyes closing again and knew he could do nothing about it. "Stay," he mumbled pleadingly but didn't remember hearing an answer.

·   ·   ·

14

The next time he woke he missed Darriel immediately, but as he opened his eyes properly and glanced over, he spotted him in the corner. He sat perched on a chair, giving one of his daughters a bottle. He opened his eyes a little wider when he saw Emmett feeding the other and Josie asleep in her car seat. He knew he hadn't made a sound, but Darriel's head jerked up as if he had and their gazes met. He had a second to absorb the tremulous smile that lightened Darriel's face before Emmett noticed and turned. His smile was wider and full of relief. "Hi, Dad. How are you feeling?"

Before he could respond, the door opened and Marco came in. He saw Zeke was awake and came right over. "You look a little better."

Which was remarkable because Zeke still felt like shit, if not as exhausted as before. "How about you tell me how I am?"

Marco glanced over at Emmett and Darriel, and Zeke understood. Taking the decision out of Zeke's hands because it could have been awkward, Marco smiled at Emmett and Darriel. "Sorry guys, but I need to talk to Zeke. Maybe go check that his room is ready?" They both stood and murmured agreement. Zeke watched as the twins were settled in the stroller. Marco held the door open. Darriel pushed the stroller out and Emmett followed, carrying Josie's car seat. He had to clamp his mouth closed to keep from telling Darriel to come back.

"Didn't they already get my room ready?" Zeke asked, sure he had heard Ryker say that.

Marco looked amused. "That was five days ago."

Zeke gaped. "I lost five days?"

"You've been in and out but I'm sure you won't remember. You had an infection serious enough that you needed IV antibiotics. You were badly beaten, and you were severely dehydrated as well. I gave you a mild sedative for the first couple of days so I could treat your back." He checked Zeke's blood pressure. "And trust me, you wouldn't have wanted to be awake for that. If you had gotten any worse, Ryker would have defied your wishes and flown you to a hospital."

Zeke huffed but didn't comment. Marco raised the bed so that Zeke was sitting up. His ribs ached but didn't scream. Zeke eagerly accepted the straw and the water Marco offered again. "Anything broken?"

"No, but you were peeing blood for a while. They did a number on you," Marco said mildly. Zeke suddenly realized what Marco wasn't asking.

"I never saw your brothers or Elena."

Marco met his gaze. "They ordered it though."

"I suppose one of them did," Zeke acknowledged, "but didn't Ryker tell me he doubted Elena was even aware that Harker was holding you?" It had been Marco's turn to get kidnapped and badly beaten last month, and his brother Nicholas that had been responsible.

*Not Elena.*

And he wondered how Marco felt about that. Elena, the head of the Panther clans for most of the west coast, also happened to be Marco's mother. Not that Elena was innocent, Zeke knew she had watched as her claw had beaten Marco as punishment for a relationship he had with a human guy, a journalist. Marco, young and convinced he was in love, had revealed he was a panther shifter to his boyfriend, who had promptly tried to out him publicly for money and to advance his career. Or he would have if Elena hadn't ordered the man killed and the story buried.

He felt for Marco and hoped, really hoped, he didn't think Zeke blamed Marco for the actions of his so-called family. Marco had been silent, as if watching all these thoughts play across Zeke's face. "She's not innocent. She might not have known Nicholas was trying to influence Trina, that just makes them as bad as each other."

"How is Trina?" Marco's younger sister was a very clever girl. She'd been waiting for her fourteenth birthday so she could declare herself independent from her mother's clan. With Marco's sponsorship as a close adult relative, she'd been able to. As far as Zeke knew, the panther clans were completely different from every other type of shifter group or pack. The alpha equivalent was the head female or Panthera, and there were many varied rules for inheritance. Marco hadn't even known his sister existed until a few weeks ago when she had run away to find him. Elena wanted her daughter either dead or controlled so she wasn't forced to give up her title. Elena was an abomination as far as Zeke was concerned, even if he disagreed with how the clans were run in the first place.

Marco smiled. "Looking more grown up every time I see her." He looked at Zeke almost warily. "I completely understand how you feel about Regina, but I cannot find an ounce of fault with how she's looking after Trina."

"I know," Zeke agreed. "I know you're in an impossible situation." He reached out a hand, ignoring how he had to make the physical effort merely to lift it, and Marco shook it gently.

"Right," he said, back to medic mode. "I want to change the dressings and get you into a comfier space. Then I can get my clinic back."

Zeke refused to let Ryker carry him. He was going to get to the room two doors across the landing if it killed him. It was touch and go for a moment as they exited the clinic when the corridor seemed tilt alarmingly, but then Darriel appeared. He brushed Ryker's and Marco's hands off Zeke and slipped his arm around him. Zeke was so shocked at how much he enjoyed the feel of Darriel's arm that he didn't protest. When they got to his room, he realized he was leaning too heavily on Darriel. He shot an apologetic look at Ryker, who immediately took his other side and didn't call him on his bullheadedness. He was ridiculously grateful to ease himself back into bed.

Emmett fussed over him until Josie started crying at the same time that Fox appeared asking for Ryker, so they both left. Zeke lay back and closed his eyes, completely exhausted and ashamed of his weakness. He heard a door close and footsteps walking away. He managed to bring his hand up to his mouth to muffle the sob as a mixture of pain, shock, and sheer fucking relief threatened to overwhelm him. But he was completely unable to stop the scalding tears that stung at his eyes and threatened to fall.

"Zeke." The whisper made him jerk and he bit his lip at the sudden pain in his back. Darriel was still here. He'd thought...but then Darriel walked around the other side of his bed where there was a little more room and carefully got in. Was he dreaming? Fuck, was he *dead*? Darriel eased him close into gentle arms and pressed Zeke's head onto his shoulder; Zeke couldn't have stopped the tears then if his life had depended on it.

# Chapter Three

Darriel's throat nearly closed as he held Zeke and tried valiantly to stop his own tears from falling. Zeke had turned onto his side so he was off his poor back and had fallen asleep with his head a comforting weight on Darriel's shoulder. Darriel knew Zeke didn't remember him helping to care for him, even if it had been Ryker and Marco waking him to use a bottle to pee in, and then practically carrying him to the bathroom after three days. And all Darriel could do was give him his privacy and sit with him when he was back in bed just waiting while he slept on the heavy painkillers Marco gave him. If Kai and Charles hadn't helped him with the girls, he didn't know what he would have done. At least neither Marco nor Ryker had objected to him sitting with Zeke every moment he could.

Zeke moaned a little and Darriel automatically hummed and stroked his hair. It had been the only thing that had quieted him when he had been delirious with fever and in pain. In those moments, Zeke had still believed Trina needed help and tried to get out of bed. That had quickly become muddled with Josie and hearing Zeke cry out for his dead lover had broken Darriel's heart.

Sometime later, the door opened quietly and Fox walked in. Darriel smiled tremulously, waiting for the enforcer to object to where he was, but Fox just smiled. "Shift change," he whispered. "Go cuddle your daughters and grab some food. Marco says you need some rest."

Darriel nodded and eased gently out of the bed. He'd missed his girls over the last few days, even if he had spent every night in his own room with them. They were already developing personalities. Emmy didn't seem to understand why Daddy needed any sleep, while Karina always needed to be woken to eat. Marco had cautioned against letting them sleep right through the night originally, even if they wanted to, until they both got to six pounds. They were nearly seven weeks old now and while Emmy was seven pounds, Karina was just over six. They'd both put on weight and were eating well, and Darriel had been looking forward to sleeping through the night, but it wasn't to be.

He walked into the kitchen taking a crying Emmy from Dinah. "Because you're not a baby are you," he murmured. "You're a little monkey."

Dinah chuckled. "She's just like my Gideon. He never seemed to think he needed sleep either." Dinah turned to go help Isabelle with the cooking, so Darriel was saved from needing to reply. He knew Dinah had a son and grandbabies she never saw, but not even Emmett knew why.

He turned, smiling shyly at Charles, who was sitting at one of the dining tables with his brood of kids rescued from the pack in Columbia that had had a shootout. None of these children had parents and Charles—an omega who had been a prisoner since he was fourteen—had found a reason to live in caring for them. A win-win, as Kai said.

He soothed Emmy and she quieted. Babies weren't supposed to be able to see very far at this age, but he'd swear she was looking right at him. "You going to let Daddy get some sleep tonight, huh?"

She waved a fist at him and he chuckled. He was completely

exhausted, but almost deliriously happy because Zeke was home and safe. Even though he knew that once Zeke healed, he would leave. Then every time Zeke visited his son, Darriel would be reminded that he wasn't good enough for him. Maybe he should move away? But as soon as the thought entered his head, he dismissed it. Look at what had happened to Kai for exactly that reason. No, it would take a crowbar to get him away from here. He smiled as Dinah put a yummy-smelling bowl of soup down in front of him and some bread he knew had only just come out of the oven. "Thank you," he whispered, a little teary as Dinah hugged him.

"If she won't settle so you can eat, give me another shout. I have plenty of help in here now."

"May I?" Darriel looked up and smiled at Charles, who nodded to Emmy. "At least until you finish your soup?"

Darriel handed her over. "Thank you." And he watched as one by one all of Charles's little band sidled up to say hello to the baby. Charles was so good with all the kids. Gentle, but steady. Like he could be relied upon. He didn't know exactly what had happened between him and Kai and it wasn't any of his business, but Charles had already proven his worth here in a few short weeks.

Everyone helped. He let that thought settle a moment. *Everyone?* He didn't. He hadn't done anything since he got here. All he'd done was accept everyone else's help and pine over a man who was too good for him. *Way too good for him.*

Ryker strode into the kitchen a few minutes later and smiled at him. Darriel was just considering going for a nap, as both girls were asleep. "Do you mind relieving Fox for a few minutes? I need him."

"I'll watch the girls," Charles said immediately, so Darriel followed Ryker back to Zeke's room. Ryker pushed open the door and with a glance at the sleeping man on the bed, beckoned Fox out. Darriel didn't wait to hear what they said, he was too pleased at having the chance to see Zeke again. He immediately sat on the chair next to the bed. It was a lot comfier than the usual ones they had in the clinic.

He stared at Zeke's hands. He'd held one all week while Zeke was fevered and in pain. He really wanted to do the same now, but Zeke seemed to be asleep. It might disturb him, and he needed the sleep. Darriel sighed, still staring at the scratched and bruised hands with their broken nails. He could only imagine how they had gotten that way. He wanted so much to touch, to soothe. To feel the warm skin. Wishing Zeke wanted to feel *him*, touch *him*.

He lifted his gaze to Zeke's face and jerked a little in shock. Zeke's eyes were open and watching him. He even had the slightest crinkle to the corner of his eyes as if he was going to smile. Darriel smiled before he had even thought about it. "Hey."

Zeke's gaze dropped to Darriel's hands and Darriel followed it. They were nearly touching. So desperate to feel, he'd moved his hand across the comforter without thinking. Before he could form the thought of snatching it away, Zeke's fingers moved slightly and brushed his.

Darriel froze and raised his head back up to meet Zeke's watchful gaze. He couldn't speak. If he could have frozen this moment forever, he would have. He reached a little farther and curled his hand over Zeke's. He barely dared to look to see how Zeke was reacting, but somehow, he gathered his courage and just waited. He knew if he opened his mouth, he'd say things he shouldn't. Maybe what he wanted. But the pressure of saying *something* was too hard to resist. "You scared me." Which was the biggest understatement ever, and not what he'd been going to say at all. He was going to...what? Politely inquire as to his health?

"Sorry," Zeke croaked out. Darriel cursed himself because Zeke didn't need to apologize for anything. Darriel moved his hand and reached for the glass of water. Zeke was propped up on enough pillows that he could drink with the straw. Darriel held the glass and angled the straw. Zeke's lips parted and once more his hand landed on Darriel's, lightly covering it over the glass. Darriel could feel his useless heart skip a ridiculous extra beat. Zeke stopped sucking and

Darriel moved the glass back, missing the warmth from Zeke's hand already.

"Thank you."

Darriel smiled because somehow, he didn't think Zeke was just thanking him for the water. Zeke shuffled a little and tried unsuccessfully to hide his wince; he glanced at the IV which was still attached to his arm.

"Marco says it can come out as soon as you're drinking enough."

Zeke's smile was a little wider. "It'll be out today. I can't spend another day in bed. Too much to do." Darriel's lips parted on an objection, but he closed them, remembering he didn't have the right to tell Zeke what he could or couldn't do. "How are the girls?"

Darriel relaxed a little, confident of this subject at least. "Karina made it over the six-pound mark and Emmy's seven pounds, eight ounces."

"So, you can let them sleep through the night?"

Darriel flushed, absurdly pleased that Zeke knew what Marco had advised. He nodded. "Seven hours but Marco doesn't advise going longer than that."

"Why do you look so exhausted, then?" Zeke asked quietly.

"I—" How was he supposed to answer that? "Emmy's just cranky sometimes." He could hardly say that when they napped during the day he slipped in here. That his friends helped out so he could do so, but that at night he just had to suck up. He knew it wouldn't be for long because he wouldn't be coming in here when Zeke was healthy, but he didn't want to have to think about that.

"If—" Darriel swallowed, and his heart beat a little faster. "If Marco wants you to rest some more, I can always read to you so you're not bored. Like you did to me." *Please.* Could Zeke hear him begging? Darriel had barely been able to stand for so many weeks and this human man had taken it upon himself to keep him company. Read him stories day after day. Chat about his business. How it had started. How losing Josie had started the whole Shifter Rescue organization. He'd even told him how he'd met Ryker and saved his life. It had been utterly amazing.

And little by little Darriel—usually completely terrified of alphas, even purely human ones—had started to relax around this kind man. Started to trust him.

Started to *love* him.

It wasn't the instantaneous *true mates love* that happened between shifters even if sometimes they fought it. But it didn't make it any less powerful, or make it hurt any less when it wasn't returned. Why was he doing this? Putting himself through this? *Because he knew it had an end date.* Not that Darriel ever imagined he would love Zeke any less, but that he knew as soon as Zeke was better, he would return to his world and only occasionally return here to visit Emmett and Josie. Zeke hadn't replied to his question, so perhaps that was his answer. That Zeke was trying to find the right way to let Darriel down gently. He should go.

The door opened and Marco walked in, looking pleased when he saw Zeke was awake. "How's my star patient?"

Zeke broke eye contact with Darriel and huffed. "What makes me think you're being sarcastic?"

Marco grinned back and then glanced at Darriel. Darriel took the hint immediately and slipped from the room, barely looking at either of them.


Zeke watched him go, then after a moment realized how quiet it was. Marco was looking at him expectantly like he was waiting for an answer. When he realized Zeke clearly hadn't a clue what he had said, he smiled. "If you have no trouble drinking, I'm happy to take the IV out. You need food, though."

Zeke scrunched up his nose. "Didn't I have soup?" He seemed to remember something like that.

"Yes, a little, when Darriel could persuade you to try it."

Zeke focused on Marco, immediately suspicious. Was he being

teased? Marco shrugged. "You had a 104-degree fever. I'd sedated you to treat your back, but I didn't want to give you more. You couldn't so much as sit up without being in tremendous pain, but you kept on insisting Trina was in danger and that you had to get up. If one of us had tried to physically restrain you, you would have been hurt. Darriel was the only person who could persuade you to lie still."

Zeke felt a flush rise up his neck, glad his scruff was covering it.

"Twenty-four hours later you'd calmed down, but after helping us out I wasn't about to say to him, 'Oh, you can't visit now because we don't need you.'" Zeke didn't reply. He didn't know what to say.

He checked Zeke's temperature and blood pressure. "He's been in here most of the day, every day. Sometimes with the girls, sometimes not. The rest of us have been covering nights."

Zeke frowned. "But he said Emmy's not sleeping well."

"She's still small even though she's now a typical weight for a regular human baby. Karina's only just weighed in at six pounds, so he's continued feeding her every four hours. Babies often don't sleep even if they can, no matter how much we would wish it."

Zeke couldn't look at Marco which wasn't like him at all. "He has a kind heart."

Marco remained silent, checked his dressings and nodded approvingly. "I'm going to get Dinah to bring you some food. You need a shifter diet."

Zeke smiled even though he didn't feel like it. "Do I have to catch it myself?"

Marco chuckled. "Lots of protein. I know you want to heal, so fuel your body." He paused. "And give yourself a break, huh?"

"Meaning?" Zeke said looking up.

"Meaning you're with family. And I don't just mean Emmett. It took me a long time to learn that as well." Marco left, making sure Zeke had his phone close, obviously deciding Zeke didn't need a babysitter anymore.

*Family?* It was true he'd spent more and more time here. His apartment had been occupied by Trina and May, but it was empty once more, so he could return. He used to love that place. His oasis when he needed quiet. When he needed to sleep somewhere famil- iar, not in the dozens of hotels he stayed in. So why had the thought of returning lost its appeal?

Although, he'd hardly come out of his recent experience unscathed, and he didn't mean just physically. *That must be it.* He was recovering. He'd be fine in another day and go home. It was the right thing to do.

Zeke huffed, not sure who he was trying to fool. Everyone else or himself?

# Chapter Four

D arriel stayed away from Zeke the rest of the day and it nearly killed him. He got to spend time with Kai and Emmett though, and felt less guilty because he wasn't asking someone else to watch Emmy and Karina. He took himself to bed just after the girls were both down, but then lay awake. When Emmy started fussing at two the next morning he was still awake and saw to her. He didn't mind because he needed to think about something else other than a pair of blue-gray eyes and a kind smile. After Emmy went back to sleep around four, he fell into an exhausted doze, only to be woken by Karina at seven. She had predictably slept all night, not even waking when he had fed her after Emmy in the middle of the night. He dragged himself out of bed and saw to them both.

He'd just fastened the last buckle in the stroller when a knock on the door surprised him. He opened it; Fox stood there grinning. "They want you for a meeting in an hour, but I thought you'd like to get some food first." He glanced at the stroller, grinned, and grabbed it. "Dinah's made pancakes."

Darriel followed. "Who wants me?"

"The boss. Nothing bad."

Darriel planted his feet, an idea, an urgency stopping him. "Please give me five minutes?"

He wanted to check. To give him one more chance. Zeke hadn't actually *said* he didn't want Darriel, and yesterday... Yesterday Zeke had been *different*.

Fox grinned. "I can do that," and he turned to resume propelling the stroller toward the kitchen.

Darriel rushed to Zeke's room in the other wing. He took a deep breath, then knocked gently. When he heard "come-in", he pushed the door open. He immediately zeroed on Zeke, sitting up holding a glass of water. He took in the plate with the remains of some eggs on it and smiled.

"You look better."

Zeke didn't reply. Instead, he stared at Darriel with such focus that Darriel could feel himself going hot, and that hadn't happened in...*forever*. "Emmy kept you awake last night?"

*No, you did*, but he just nodded. "Ryker wants me at some meeting, but I wondered if you'd thought about the books? I can go choose some for after. If the girls are asleep," he added.

"If the girls are asleep, so should you be," Zeke said in a scolding tone that made Darriel's heart dance a little. He sounded like he cared.

"It's okay, I—"

But Zeke was shaking his head. "You need to concentrate on you and those babies. You don't need to be running around after me."

Darriel processed the words but waited, unsure of what they meant. They could be concern, or—

"I'm getting up today. If Marco gives me the green light, I'll go back home."

*Home.* Somewhere different. Somewhere Darriel wasn't. And it hurt so much even though he was expecting it. But Darriel simply smiled his agreement, mumbled something, and turned and left.

If he spent the next five minutes standing in the empty hallway unable to move, shaking, and trying really hard not to cry, it didn't matter. No one saw anyway. *At least I have my answer.*

He took a deep breath and headed into the kitchen and over to the "Omega Club corner" as Emmett had christened it. Kai was already there with Emmett. Dinah met him as he came in.

"How did they sleep?"

"Not bad," Darriel murmured vaguely, bending down and scooping up Emmy, who was starting to fuss. Dinah did the same with Karina. As soon as Emmy quieted, Darriel looked up to find Emmett and Kai staring at him expectantly.

"I'm going to visit with my dad while you're all in the meeting," Emmett said. "He looked tons better this morning."

Darriel wasn't sure what reply Emmett was expecting and tried to ignore the deep hurt in his chest. "Good idea." He knew Emmett wanted to spend time with Zeke. They had swapped shifts over the past few days. Sometimes they had both sat quietly with the babies. Emmett hadn't once objected to Darriel's presence. In fact, it had been Emmett who had gone to find him that first day. He'd said that he and Dinah would take care of the girls so Darriel could go see Zeke.

Darriel had stood outside the closed clinic door that day for what seemed like forever before Marco had opened it, smiled at him, and said, "Thanks. I need to go speak with May and check Zeke's medical history so I can order the antibiotics. Can you watch him for me until I get back?"

And Darriel had been so grateful. Marco might have been a panther shifter, but he was the equivalent of a werewolf alpha. He knew Marco would have heard or smelled him as he approached the clinic. Darriel had practically crept into the room to see Zeke positioned on his side to keep the pressure off his back. Emmett had told him about all of Zeke's injuries and he'd struggled not to cry. He'd sat on the stool next to Zeke's bed and gazed at his pale face, sunken cheeks, and bruises. So *many* bruises. The first time Zeke had moaned in distress, Darriel had taken his hand, which had seemed to settle him. He'd never wanted to let go after that.

"What meeting?" Kai asked, taking a gulp of orange juice. Pulled back from the memory, Darriel glanced at Emmett. He'd been so focused on talking to Zeke that he hadn't even thought about what Fox had told him.

"Something to do with Mills River," Emmett said. "Morgan, Jered's beta, is coming over."

"But why would they need to talk to me?" Darriel asked. Emmett settled a sleeping Josie back in her stroller and stood up.

"It's probably just to see if you remember someone."

Darriel leaned back and cuddled his daughter, staring at the baby he never thought he'd hold, remembering the ones he had lost. He was forever grateful to Ryker and the rest of this pack for giving him a life. He shouldn't be greedy and want more. Besides, he knew that Zeke would probably leave today. Darriel bent down to kiss Emmy, inhaling her baby smell and trying cover the stab to his heart as he acknowledged the words. It was a good thing Zeke was human. If they had been shifter mates and he rejected Darriel, Darriel could have gotten sick, and he had two people relying on him now that he had to stay healthy for. He'd struggled while Zeke was missing, but he kept going for his daughters. And that wasn't going to change.

He had friends. He had a home. He had two precious babies who were utter miracles. There was no point wishing for things he couldn't have. It was selfish.

An hour later, the girls had both been fed and put back in their stroller. Chrissy appeared and asked, "Can you come to the meeting?"

Kai looked up from where he was cuddling Elliot. "They can stay here with me. Dinah or one of the others will help if I need it."

"I think Charles is on his way with the brood as well," Chrissy said, smiling. Darriel got up nervously and followed her. Every other time they'd needed to know if he remembered someone from Mills River, Ryker had come to him. He'd never been summoned to a meeting before, especially with Mills River's new beta commander, who—if rumors were true—was more than a friend to the new alpha.

Darriel stood stock-still outside the room for a second. Were they going to tell him he had to go back? *Surely not...* Darriel almost whimpered at the thought of having to give up his home and his new family. Ryker could make him go back and Darriel would have no choice. Was that it? Was that what they were going to say?

"Darriel?"

Chrissy's words finally registered through his panic, and he flushed as he got the impression it wasn't the first time she had addressed him. He hurriedly stepped into the room, feeling every wolf glance at him.

Ryker stood, smiling, and met Darriel at the door, leading him to the seat next to him. "It's okay. We just need to ask you if you remember someone. Don't worry."

Darriel leaned close to his alpha, taking comfort from his assurance. "Darriel, this is Morgan." Ryker continued. "He's Jered's—the new alpha of Mills River—right-hand man and beta commander." Darriel peeked at him. He had to be careful because in Darriel's experience a lot of alphas didn't like it when omegas looked them in the face, and the ones who thought they should be alphas were a million times worse. Beta commander also meant he had many betas reporting to him.

Morgan smiled reassuringly. That and being close to Ryker's side helped his heart settle a little. The beta was older than he'd expected, especially as he knew the new alpha was only in his twenties. But he guessed it made sense for a young alpha to seek advice from someone with more experience.

Ryker turned to Morgan. "Now that we're all here, what can we do for you?" Darriel nearly gaped at Ryker. He'd made it sound like it was important that they waited for him. Like he mattered. Darriel didn't know what to think of that. It had been a long time since he had been important to anyone.

But before Morgan could answer, the door opened and everyone turned to see Zeke hobble into the room, followed closely by Fox. Ryker grinned and pulled out the chair on the other side of him. "About time you got your lazy ass out of bed."

Everyone laughed. Except Darriel. Darriel was too shocked to make a sound. He remembered to drag his gaze away so no one would see him staring and swallowed down the lump in his throat. He only looked up again when Zeke was sitting and Morgan started talking.

"I understand you recently bought a parcel of land to the west of your pack. I know it doesn't have the national park access, but as you can use the pack areas you have already, that doesn't matter." Morgan paused as if waiting for Ryker to agree.

"Yes, we're going to get increasingly short of space and the area, though large, isn't anywhere near the human hunting areas. We're hoping to develop pack housing on a more individual basis. There are families that would like a little land they can cultivate."

Morgan chuckled. "You have to be the only shifter pack I know of that has wolves wanting to grow vegetables."

Ryker grinned back. "It's more about being self-sufficient. Some of the pack don't want to be seen."

Because they'd been through a similar experience as he had, Darriel thought. There was an omega named Louis who was so traumatized he wouldn't even interact with the other omegas, but oddly enough Sam, their new beta, had been able to talk to him.

"I also understand you met with Paxton and Porter Davies yesterday and they're threatening legal action to get it back."

Darriel felt his alpha still and knew instinctively Ryker didn't like the beta from another pack—as friendly as they were—knowing his movements. Morgan sighed. "You should know that we have heard some disturbing reports about the brothers. Nothing we can prove yet, but our information came from another pack member. It's reliable enough that we thought you should know. One of our betas heard chatter about the 'hippy commune' being set up here and that they'd said everyone had better make sure their doors were locked. My alpha instructed me to find out exactly what the brothers meant and it wasn't difficult." Darriel watched Ryker relax a little.

"What sort of disturbing reports?"

Darriel glanced at Red. His voice had taken on a hard edge. He was generally easy-going, or so Darriel thought. Although, since he'd never been included in a security meeting, maybe this wasn't unusual. Then he saw Chrissy's face flicker with surprise.

Morgan passed a couple of photos over to Ryker. Darriel glanced down at them and frowned.

"You know the Davies brothers?" Ryker asked, indicating the two photographs.

"Not the older man, but this one." Darriel tapped the second picture.

"How do you know Porter?" Morgan asked.

Darriel wrinkled his nose in concentration. "I didn't really. I didn't know his name. He once came to Riggs's cabin while I was there." Darriel tried not to dwell on the memory, thankfully hazy after what Riggs had given him.

"Riggs met a full human at his cabin?" Red queried. "On pack lands?"

"He just turned up. I don't think anyone else was with him."

"Where was this cabin?" Morgan asked. "Was it the one next to your omega house?"

"Riggs had another one." Darriel swallowed thickly. "He'd take me there when he needed somewhere quiet."

The scrape from Zeke's chair seemed very loud in the silence that followed, but no one said a word. They all knew what "somewhere quiet" meant.

"Why was he meeting these guys?" Ryker broke the silence. "Riggs was a bastard, but he knew better than to bring humans onto shifter land, surely?"

Morgan scrubbed his face and passed over another photograph. Ryker frowned and showed it to Red so quickly Darriel didn't get a glimpse, but everyone in the room heard the warning rumble from

Red's throat. Ryker didn't respond, he simply took the photo back and showed it to Darriel.

Darriel stared at the young man. He looked very familiar. "I knew him or someone who looked a lot like him."

"Who is he?" Ryker asked.

"If it's the same person, his name is Bodhi."

"Not Bobby?" Red asked carefully.

"No, Bodhi. I can't be certain because it was quite a few years ago, when I was sent to the omega house. He was one of the ones already there. He wasn't there long."

"Do you know why?" Ryker asked.

"Omegas changed all the time. We were never told why and none of us dared talk about it, certainly not in front of any of the gammas. I just woke up one day and he wasn't there."

Morgan cleared his throat. "From what we can find out, this is Bobby Davies, Porter's son. According to public record, his mother was a Jane Smith. She died in a road traffic accident ten years ago and Bobby went to live with a cousin, Porter, who then legally adopted him. His name was recorded as Bobby."

"I haven't had time to do much about this—" He shot an apologetic look at Zeke. "But the day we met, Porter ordered him to pass me the envelope from the lawyers. He took one look at me and practically froze in fear. I have no idea why. We've certainly never met. I definitely caught a shifter scent, but Red didn't. Since it wasn't something I could identify, I thought I could be wrong. Having said that, Red and I were both uncomfortable because he had visible bruises, so I asked May to look into things for me."

"Which she did," Zeke interrupted, "and that's why I'm here. I spoke to her a little while ago. Unsurprisingly, Jane Smith never existed despite the ID the cops found. Apart from his birth certificate it looks like Bobby Smith didn't exist before that point either, which seems suspicious."

"If it is Bodhi, he probably only ever remembers living in the omega house," Darriel confirmed. "He said he was told he didn't have a mom or a dad. He knew he wasn't a wolf, but he didn't know anything else. And he learned not to ask questions."

*Like me.* Darriel knew he hadn't said the words out loud, but he felt like he'd shouted them. Ryker brushed their arms together and Darriel breathed in the scent of his alpha. It gave him the strength to look up.

"Which fits with what we've found out as well," Morgan said. "According to our records, he is registered as a mixed breed but specifics aren't mentioned. The ages fit, if this is the same person."

"He—" Darriel stopped but then remembered he wasn't *there* anymore and carried on. "We were all treated...well, you know. But Bodhi was terrified. He had these panic attacks. Would stop breathing. He was worse when the alpha came."

"Which might explain his fear, if he scented me as an alpha," Ryker acknowledged.

"So, let me see if I've got this right," Chrissy butted in. "You *think* there's an orphaned shifter, but we don't know what type of shifter. He disappeared from Mills River and ended up with his supposed human cousin who adopted him. This same cousin we *know* turned up to see Riggs at some point. And now they have randomly crossed paths with us?"

Ryker nodded acknowledging Chrissy's point.

"What did your pack member tell you?" Zeke asked. Darriel risked a look at him. Pale but determined. He was probably in pain, but he wouldn't show it. Not that Darriel could do anything for him even if he did.

Morgan rubbed a hand over his eyes. "This is going to sound crazy but bear with me?"

No one responded, simply listened. "All the gammas of my alpha's uncle were either killed or ran after the challenge, except one. Deke Robson. He was one of the record keepers, and apart from that, he never got involved. He knew what was going on and didn't try to stop it, but as far as we know he never physically abused an omega." Morgan glanced at Darriel.

"I've never heard of him."

Morgan seemed to be relieved. "He took a gunshot to the head during the challenge. The wound healed, but somehow it interfered with him being able to shift. After experiencing severe debilitating headaches because he couldn't shift, he basically shut himself off in one of the outlying cabins. He has a daughter who is mated to one of our betas who was allowed to visit with meals, but he wouldn't have much to do with her apart from that. Anyway, a week ago Honey goes to take him some supper to find he'd blown his brains out with an old shotgun."

Darriel listened, knowing there was something else coming. Morgan wouldn't have come all the way here only to report who they thought Bodhi might be. If that were the case, he would have just given Ryker a call.

"Honey found some old, handwritten ledgers. She handed them over in case we needed them. One contained a note about 'special sales.' There are three different recorded payments. The first just says the name Bodhi and a notation of fi5,000. In pencil the initials PD are written next to it. The other two names are Roe with the initials VK, and Shiloh with the initials DW."

Ryker leaned forward. "You're assuming these are omegas who have been sold?"

Before Morgan could answer, Zeke interjected. "But even if Bodhi and Bobby are the same person, and PD stands for Porter Davies, why would a human buy an omega? Assuming he knew what one was of course."

"Agreed," Ryker said.

"We don't know. I came here because I know you two—" Morgan nodded at Zeke and Ryker "—can get information we can't. And to be honest, we have no records of either a Roe or a Shiloh. Asking about them will take some time. Aggie, our pack mother, confirmed we have had no pups born with either name in the last thirty years."

Darriel believed him. He knew that some of the gifted pack

mothers could remember the name of every pup they'd ever delivered.

The meeting broke up after that. Darriel watched Morgan shake hands with everyone. He even came to Darriel and held out his hand. Darriel took it in astonishment. It was such an un-wolflike thing to do in the first place, but then to afford him the same respect as his alpha was staggering. Morgan smiled. "My alpha couldn't come today, but he wanted me to pass on the apologies of Mills River for your treatment by our pack. If you ever need anything, please know you can call us."

For a moment he was so tempted to ask if he could go back. What would it be like not having to see what he couldn't have all the time? As Morgan walked away, he stood to go, knowing he needed to see to the girls, but before he could leave, he felt a hand on his arm. He knew who it was immediately. He looked up into Zeke's eyes.

"Can we talk?"

Darriel scoffed out a hurt sound. Talk? He didn't need to talk. He'd gotten the message loud and clear. "You don't have anything to say that I want to hear." And he fairly bolted out of the room.

# Chapter Five

Zeke stared at the empty space Darriel had just occupied and watched as everyone filed out. None of the shifters said anything to him. Hell, none of them even looked at him. When the last one had left, he wobbled and grabbed the chair arm. Fox hadn't even waited to make sure he could get back to his room.

"Well, you screwed that up."

Zeke glanced back at Ryker standing with his arms folded, cursing that he hadn't even realized he'd stayed behind. It made sense though. Zeke lowered himself slowly into the chair again and met his friend's cool gaze. Or almost met it. Zeke wasn't a shifter, but he understood alphas and pack dynamics. At the moment, he wasn't looking at his friend, he was looking at Darriel's alpha.

"He came to see me this morning and he looked exhausted. I know Emmy's not sleeping and he's not napping when the girls do, he's coming to see me instead." Zeke shook his head. "He's making himself sick, Ryker. Have you noticed how much weight he's lost?"

Ryker huffed out a breath and dropped into the chair next to Zeke. "I saw. But he's as much of a stubborn ass as you. Emmett's worried sick about him. Dinah's struggling to get him to eat." He paused. "I don't think this is just about the babies."

Zeke closed his eyes, feeling wretched. He'd taken advantage. Marco had told him how much Darriel had been there. "What would you have me do? He can't saddle himself with an old man, an old *human* man."

Ryker scoffed. "You ain't old, but aside from that, let me ask you something I've stayed out of ever since we met. Is this about Emmett's mom?"

Zeke swallowed. Even up to a year ago, Zeke would have told Ryker it was none of his business. He'd told Ryker who and what she was, of course. More details since he had discovered Emmett was the son he never knew about, but he'd never discussed how he felt about her. Why would he? He had barely talked about her with Emmett, just that they'd been in love and Josie had left because of the threat to Zeke's life. Because panther shifters weren't allowed to mate other shifter species, never mind humans. As it had turned out, Regina, Emmett's grandmother and the head of her panther clan, didn't feel like that—now or then—or so she said, anyway.

A tiny sliver of doubt wormed its way in. He remembered what his jailers had taunted him with. He knew Regina had proven she could be trusted with Emmett and Josie, but what if she hadn't really changed and was just turning a blind eye because of her grandson?

"What was that thought?"

Zeke smiled ruefully at Ryker. "Can we really trust Regina?"

Ryker frowned. "Is this your way of telling me to mind my own business?"

"Maybe. I don't know." Zeke rubbed his aching head. "It's kind of all mixed up together."

"Then let's take one thing at a time."

"Darriel," Zeke acknowledged. "I'm not a shifter."

"Neither was my mom," Ryker said bluntly.

Zeke's head jerked up. Shit. He'd forgotten that. "I didn't mean —" He stopped. What did he mean? "I meant that he's young and should have a mate. A proper one. Someone who understands all this." He waved a hand around vaguely.

Ryker nodded. "You mean shifter society? Their needs? Pack dynamics?"

"Yes," Zeke said, grateful Ryker got it.

"I can see how that would be a problem," Ryker continued slowly as if he was considering everything. "He would need someone who was close to a pack. Who had lived among shifter society for a lot of years. Who understood pack politics more than most shifters. Who had *mated* a shifter. Who had a shifter *son*. Who had *fought* for more omegas and vulnerable shifters than any alpha I've ever known. Who puts his money where his mouth is. *Every. Damn. Day.*"

Zeke didn't even bother with a reply. He didn't have one.

"You are one of the most intelligent men I have ever met. Why are you being so damn stupid?" Ryker sighed in apparent frustration. "I'll go back to my original question. Are you denying Darriel because you are still in love with Josephine? Because if that's why, I'll back off right here, right now."

Zeke was tempted to lie, but he couldn't. He'd loved Josie with all his heart, but it had been a long time ago. He shook his head, completely unable to speak past the lump in his throat.

"Next question then. If you didn't consider yourself too old. If he wasn't a shifter. Would you have rejected Darriel?"

"I—It's not that simple," Zeke croaked out.

"Yeah, buddy," Ryker put a hand on his shoulder. "Sometimes it is."

"How do I know it's not just because he's grateful?" He'd turned up in a stupid ass helicopter to bring him here.

"You don't."

Zeke winced. *Not* the answer he'd been hoping for.

"How do I know Emmett loves me for me and not just because I'm the alpha?"

Zeke scoffed. Emmett adored Ryker. Even he could see that.

Ryker just arched an eyebrow. Zeke answered it with an annoyed look.

"Although he does have a couple of kids that aren't yours," Ryker acknowledged.

"As if that—" Zeke bit off his outraged reply, knowing he'd just played right into Ryker's hands.

Ryker nodded. "As to your second question, yes."

"What?" Zeke frowned trying to remember what else he'd asked Ryker.

"Yes, I trust Regina. I don't agree with their society, but Regina cannot change hundreds of years of culture in the space of a few years. She has to prioritize and at the moment she needs the clan backing on the shifter council. There's a chance she might be asked to join now and we need her there. She called it on where Marco was. I was given two locations, if you remember. If she hadn't pointed out how impossible it was for a regular shifter to know how to contact the shifter council, Marco would likely be dead. And Kai would be back with Samson and wishing he was."

Zeke closed his eyes, exhaustion snapping at him. He'd felt tons better this morning. After he'd had the call from May, he'd even managed to get back on his feet and come to the meeting. Now he wasn't certain he could even stand. "You think we should tell Regina?"

Ryker inclined his head, understanding the subject of Darriel was firmly closed for now. "I think we're out of our depth here."

Zeke knew he was. "And the Davies brothers?"

"As far as I'm aware, the only shifter not identifiable by scent is a panther. But as you know, that's zero scent, as in he or she would be mistaken for a human. There was definitely *something*. He was enough of a shifter with what had to be assumed omega physiology to be identified by the pack mother and sent to the omega house at Mills River. Although Darriel said Bodhi was there before him, and no one has managed to find any records on him. For all we know, the shifter that Darriel met and Bobby could be two different people. You heard

Darriel yourself. There were a lot of omegas who passed through there."

"What can I do to help?"

"Get well. I'm about to help you back to bed."

Zeke stiffened. He—

"And don't give me that. Fox has cleared the corridor and is outside waiting for us. If I have to carry you I will."

"You're a sneaky bastard," Zeke grumbled, but it was all for show. He knew it and Ryker knew it. He managed to stand, but it was only by leaning on Ryker that he got back to his room. Ryker shut the blinds and Zeke closed his eyes. He didn't even remember Ryker leaving.


When he woke, Zeke's first thought was of Darriel, and he knew he was no further on answering Ryker's question. He looked at his phone and almost shook it thinking it had stopped. One a.m.? What the hell? How had he slept for nine hours? He got up gingerly, his bladder immediately confirming the time frame, and he hobbled to the bathroom. The dressings were off now, and he desperately needed a shower, so after he'd emptied his bladder with a considerable amount of relief, he stripped. He even ignored the pull on his skin to raise his arms and shampoo his hair. When he was out and dried, he acknowledged he felt hungry for the first time since he got back and decided to go raid Dinah's large fridge in the kitchen. He knew she kept it stocked all the time for hungry shifters, and he could definitely eat.

After helping himself to some pasta salad and glugging two glasses of water, he felt tons better. Almost normal. He'd go back and get his laptop out and do some work. Anything to avoid thinking about what he'd talked about with Ryker, or more importantly, *who* he'd talked about.

He cleaned up and head back to his room. He stopped for a moment before he left and glanced back to the other side of the kitchen. Towards the omega rooms. Was Darriel getting some rest? A faint sound made him pause. Then it got louder. Definitely a crying baby. He followed the noise. By the time he got closer, the wailing was loud. Without hesitation he pushed open the door and jerked to a stop.

Darriel looked up. Zeke took in Emmy screaming at the top of her voice, the tears that were running down Darriel's cheek, and Karina who was awake and whimpering in her crib. "Has she eaten?"

Darriel nodded miserably. "An hour ago. Chrissy helped, but I sent her back to bed. Charles came in, but I can't keep relying on others, they're my responsibility."

Zeke stepped up to Darriel and held his hands out confidently. "Give me this little imp. You see to Karina." Zeke wasn't sure which one of them was more surprised, Emmy or him, when Darriel handed her over. "Diaper?"

"Just changed," Darriel said, the surprise clear in his voice. Zeke almost laughed. Did Darriel think he got servants to look after Josie when he took her for a few hours to give Emmett a rest?

Karina quieted the second Darriel picked her up, so Zeke focused on Emmy. "Now young lady, how about you tell me all about it." He went to the corner where there was a very comfy chair next to a bin holding an assortment of squishy toys and rattles. He noted with interest a couple of books on a low shelf that he had loaned Darriel even after he had stopped reading them to him. He sat down, carefully arranged Emmy, handed her a teething ring she could grip—which immediately headed to her mouth—picked up a book and started at Chapter One.

He kept glancing down at her, changing toys occasionally, but for a seven-week-old baby she seemed pretty alert. A lot noisier than Josie certainly, but if Emmy'd had the undivided attention of two adults how would she have responded? It was interesting. Ryker had a pack to run, but Zeke knew for a fact he wouldn't just laze around while Emmett got up with Josie. Same with Marco and Kai. Two babies but also two adults each. Darriel was the other way around.

One adult with two babies. One *stressed* adult with two babies. Were babies like some animals? He knew dogs and horses could sense the emotions of their owners. And shifter babies were more aware even if they didn't understand what they were sensing. It was fascinating. He chuckled at Emmy. "Your namesake's momma would have called me a dork."

He froze, immediately realizing what he'd said. He glanced up at Darriel to see his reaction, but the other man was just barely keeping his eyes open and didn't seem to have registered what Zeke had said. Karina was asleep and Darriel should be. "Why don't you put her down and get into bed. We're okay here."

Darriel swallowed. "But you need your sleep."

"I've just woken up. I fell asleep after the meeting, so I'm good. Are you hungry?"

Darriel shook his head firmly, settled Karina, and got back into bed. He didn't close his eyes though, so Zeke returned his attention to Emmy and the book. In another five minutes, Emmy's eyes were closed. He finished the chapter before looking across at Darriel, who was also asleep. Zeke put the book back and slowly retrieved the teething ring from Emmy. He stood and walked to the crib. After he settled Emmy, he kissed both babies, then turned to gaze at Darriel. The shadows under his eyes were apparent even on his brown skin. He'd been way too thin when Zeke had first seen him at Mills River, but he'd put on weight since. Now he was heading back the wrong way. Was it Zeke's fault?

He stared at the sleeping man for far too long while he was trying to work out his feelings. Ryker had asked him how he would have felt if they were both human. There was still the age gap. While that worked for some couples, twenty years was a huge difference. And he wasn't a shifter. Which meant he would age faster, even if what Marco said was true and the bond meant he would live as long as Darriel. What did that mean? Would he get to ninety and just stay there for another thirty years until Darriel caught up? What a horrendous thought, to tie down such a beautiful, vital man. Sex wouldn't be an issue because Zeke had always been bi, but as they were never going to even get that far, it didn't matter.

If he took all the objections out like Ryker had said, what did he feel? *How* did he feel? He remembered waking up at some point in the clinic utterly terrified because he thought Trina had been caught. That he'd been beaten so badly he'd succumbed and helped them find her. That he hadn't been strong enough to withstand what they had done. Even though he hadn't done anything, he'd been forced to agree with some of it. A lot of it. He did blame the clan system for Josie's death but admitting it to the man who had beaten him made him feel ashamed. Like he had given in. Like he had betrayed his son.

Was that the problem? Was that the reason he didn't feel worthy of love? Worthy of Darriel? Ryker had told him to separate everything but that was impossible. If he gave in and acted selfishly enough to mate Darriel, what would happen when Zeke became an old man and was no longer be able to protect him?

Not that he really could protect him now. Even the older kids in the pack could best him strength and speed wise.

Josie had known that. She had known that Zeke couldn't match up to a shifter. Couldn't protect her. Couldn't keep her safe. That's why she had left him. She had run away because he wasn't strong enough, and she had died.

At some point, maybe not soon, but in ten years, maybe fifteen, Darriel would realize that. Then he would leave too.

And Zeke wouldn't survive that a second time.

# Chapter Six

Darriel opened his eyes to sunlight for the first time in a long time and it took him a moment to work out why. He shot up in bed and glanced over at the cribs. When he saw that both girls were fine, *breathing*, his heart began to return to normal. Then he remembered Zeke. He had been wonderful with Emmy, with him. He had fallen asleep to the sound of that deep voice reading one of his favorite books. Or not exactly his book, but Zeke had said he could keep it because he had another.

He wasn't sure he believed him because who had two copies of the same book? Maybe he was just being kind. Darriel glanced over at the girls again and knew they'd be waking up soon, so he rushed into the bathroom and grabbed a quick shower. He could shave later. When he was dressed, he made the bottles and picked up Karina, changing her diaper. Of course, by this time Emmy was awake and wanted instant attention.

He heard the knock on the door and tried not to be disappointed when Charles poked his head in. "I was just walking past and heard them. Need an extra pair of hands?"

"Please," Darriel agreed gratefully. "Do you mind—" But Charles was already telling Emmy she was a "good girl" and asking "oh, do you need a new diaper" and "let's get you comfy and ready for breakfast," so Darriel shut up and looked down at Karina. Huge brown eyes stared at him.

"You're a good girl too, huh? She's so patient," Darriel shared, and Charles beamed, happiness rolling off him. It was so good to see. He glanced at Charles when he began snapping Emmy's onesie closed. They both settled down to feed the girls, and he asked, "How are you feeling?"

"Like I'm the luckiest man alive." Charles grinned. "I actually snuck out while the kids were finishing chores. Dinah is there and apparently the little ones are going to make cookies for the older ones when they get out of school." Charles chuckled at Emmy, who seemed to be trying to grab the bottle. "How are you doing?"

Darriel met Charles's gaze. They both shared a similar history except Charles had gone through torment for much longer. Darriel sighed. "Wanting something I can't have." Charles's eyes widened and Darriel didn't know which one of them was more surprised at his honesty. He hadn't meant to say anything.

"Is this to do with a certain human alpha?" Charles's eyes twinkled.

Darriel bit his lip. "He's not interested."

"Because?" Charles prompted.

"Because I'm not good enough for him," Darriel said morosely. "He's..." But there weren't enough words to describe how gorgeous Zeke was.

"Be more specific."

Darriel huffed. "He's a lot older than me, a businessman."

"So the age thing bothers you?"

"What?" Darriel shook his head. "No, I mean it bothers him."

Charles cocked his head. "Isn't it usually the other way around, though?"

"But—" Darriel started objecting then stopped as Charles's words sank in.

"Has he actually said you're too young for him?"

"No. But I could tell I was annoying him." Zeke hadn't been able to get rid of Darriel fast enough that morning.

"What did he say?"

"He said I should lie down while Emmy slept and not be worrying about him. He said I looked tired."

Charles arched an eyebrow. "That sounds like concern to me. Plus, he's correct. You look wrung out." Darriel didn't reply. "Have you seen him since?"

Darriel nodded and told Charles about Zeke trying to talk to him after the meeting and about last night. "But he is still in love with Emmett's mom. And even if he wasn't, I'm a guy." That mattered more to a lot of humans.

Charles nodded seriously. "He seems to be trying to spend time with you. Why don't you let him and see what happens?"

"And when he goes back to his life?"

"Then you'll know."

Darriel gazed down at Karina. "But won't that be worse?"

Charles shrugged. "What if you're wrong? What if he thinks as an older man, especially a non-shifter, that there's no way you would be interested in him? What if he's just trying to protect himself for when you leave him for a younger guy?"

Darriel gaped. "I would never—*oh*." He flushed. Maybe Charles had a point. Did he dare?

"You'll be no worse off," Charles pointed out.

Darriel nodded and eased Karina onto his shoulder, patting her back. Charles stood and put a sleeping Emmy in the stroller. "I'd better go. Mo's still really clingy."

"Did I hear Marco say he thought he'd found someone to talk to him?" Human kids would be able to go to therapy, but they hadn't found anyone they could trust for the shifter kids.

"One of the rangers he used to work with knows about us. Trusted human. His dad's a retired pediatrician. Not a therapist, but Marco can't find anyone who has ever heard Mo speak, so he wants to rule out a physical cause as well. I think Ryker was going to talk to Zeke about it. See if they dare risk it."

Charles gave Darriel a brief hug and made him promise to call if he needed help, then he left. Darriel decided to go to the kitchen and grab some food. He was actually hungry, and it was a good feeling.

He pushed the stroller over to the OC corner, although only Emmett was there and not the usual three or four others. He looked up from his phone. "Did Ryker talk to you?"

Darriel shook his head and said teasingly, "What did I do wrong this time?"

Emmett smirked and leaned forward. "What do you call a wolf that works as a lumberjack?"

Darriel groaned. Emmett's jokes were getting worse. "I don't know," he said obediently. "What *do* you call a wolf who works as a lumberjack?"

"A *timber* wolf," Emmett crowed and set off giggling. Darriel rolled his eyes but grinned.

"Why does Ryker want me?"

"Secret espionage." Emmett nodded thoughtfully.

It took Darriel a minute then he scoffed. "James Bond stuff, huh?" But before Emmett could make a comeback, Isabelle put down a plate containing something that smelled absolutely amazing.

"What's that?" Darriel asked weakly.

"Steak parcels," Isabelle smiled. "All the protein you need, wrapped up in a pretty package."

Darriel thanked Isabelle and managed to stay polite and respectful despite Emmett hyperventilating because he was trying not to laugh. Isabelle just rolled her eyes and muttered something about "boys" before she left. Darriel kicked Emmett, but it didn't help.

"How old are you?" he asked in exasperation even as he felt his lips try their best to curve into a grin despite himself.

"Three, possibly four sometimes," a dry voice intoned to their left and Emmett looked up, squealed like he hadn't seen Ryker in years and flung himself into his mate's arms. Darriel laughed because *of course*, but the accompanying harsh squeeze to his insides reminded him he didn't have that. *Pathetic, much?*

Ryker put a flushed and very thoroughly kissed Emmett down, then fixed his gaze on Darriel. "Sorry, we need you again."

Darriel glanced at the stroller, then at Emmett.

"I've got them. *We've* got them." He nodded to the door as Charles came in with the little ones. Maisie and Dinah followed them. Darriel nodded, stood, resisted the temptation to kiss Emmy and Karina because they were asleep, and followed his alpha.

Zeke sat quietly listening to the others talk around him. He was still tired, but pleasantly so. His back ached not because of the wounds, but as if he had done too many leg presses in his morning routine. He was healing nicely. Another day and he could go home. There was nothing stopping him from calling his pilot today. He could be at the office in an hour.

He ignored the desolate feelings that accompanied his thoughts and glanced at the door as it swung open. His mind briefly registered Ryker, but all his focus was on the utterly beautiful man who followed him. He frowned. Why was Darriel here? If someone else was watching the girls, he should be resting. But all thoughts left his brain when Darriel looked up, met his gaze, and *smiled.*

Zeke felt like he'd been sucker punched. It was fleeting, but Darriel had looked...at *him*. It was probably because Zeke had helped last night. Must be. But—

"Zeke, do you want to tell everyone what May found out?"

Reluctantly, Zeke dragged his eyes away from Darriel and tried to focus on the question. "Yes." He grabbed his phone with the email from May. "They want to meet again."

"Who?" Fox asked.

"The Davies brothers. Apparently, they have an alternate suggestion to avoid litigation."

Chrissy rolled her eyes. "I just bet they do." She paused incredulously. "And you believe them?"

"Absolutely not," Ryker put in. "But this might be a chance to find out what else is going on."

"You mean with Bodhi," Red said quietly. Zeke glanced in his direction. The man was Ryker's right-hand man, *wolf*, whatever. He remembered when Red used to tease Ryker about being alpha, but one time a look from Ryker had shut him up. Zeke didn't think it was because Red was intimidated. They seemed to have a deep respect for each other. He knew Ryker had been running with Red for a long time. They'd both been lone wolves and he supposed technically that made Red his first pack member.

"How will it help though?" Chrissy said. "Even if Bodhi or *Bobby* is there it's not like we're going to get the chance to talk to him. Plus, you said he was terrified. He won't go near one of us."

"Take me." Everyone in the room focused on Darriel.

Ryker looked apologetic. "Actually, that was what I was hoping you might say."

"Absolutely not," Zeke interrupted. "There's no way he can put himself at risk like that." What the fuck was Ryker thinking? Those bastards carried guns!

"We will all be there," Ryker said evenly. "In fact, as my business partner it is entirely appropriate for you to be there as well." Ryker arched an eyebrow as if daring him to say anything else.

Darriel glanced at him. "There's a good chance I'll recognize him, or my wolf will."

Zeke couldn't answer that one. *Because you're not a shifter*, he thought. He knew even with a dormant wolf that couldn't shift, Darriel still had a lot of the abilities of one.

It was agreed that the meeting would be arranged through Zeke. They wanted to meet in the same place as last time.

"Why do they want to meet in the middle of a field?" Red asked suddenly. "I mean, that's weird, isn't it? Wouldn't you expect offices?"

"I thought about that after you told me," Zeke said. "Lack of witnesses. You said they were hoping to impress you with their firepower."

"It still seems odd, though," Ryker agreed. He shrugged. "And there's nowhere for anyone to hide. I suppose in the middle of a field we can't hide wolves."

Ryker's eyes widened the second he'd said it as did Zeke's.

"Shit," Red exclaimed, obviously working out the same thing.

"What's wrong?" Darriel asked.

"Because it implies they know we're shifters," Ryker ground out. "If they wanted to intimidate humans, they would have picked a swanky lawyer's office, not meet in the middle of a field with guns."

"You think Riggs told him?" Chrissy asked. "It seems odd that Darriel saw him unchallenged on shifter land. Even in a remote cabin he should have had sentries picking up on his scent."

Ryker swore. "It should have occurred to me then."

"It didn't occur to any of us," Red nearly spat out, standing and stalking to the window. Zeke watched him. Red was usually pretty easygoing. Something had him riled up. Had Zeke missed something?

Darriel leaned forward. "Are you saying you think that's somehow the reason that Porter has Bodhi? Because he knows what he is?"

Ryker scrubbed a hand over his face. "The trouble is, we don't even know what he is. I could definitely sense shifter, but not what kind and that bothers me."

"I've never asked this before," Zeke said slowly. "But what other shifter species are there?"

Ryker gazed at Chrissy. "Wolves, panthers, bears, bobcats, leopards."

"Tigers, but as far as we know they are extinct," Chrissy added.

"Same with lions. Although I can't swear there might not be some mountain lion packs. The thing is, they withdrew from shifter society completely some years ago, so I have no idea."

"Plus, we don't know what there is worldwide," Fox added.

"Regina may know more," Ryker said.

"No foxes," Fox said in some amusement.

"Except sly ones," Chrissy shot back, and the mood lightened a little.

"Elk," Ryker said slowly as if he was thinking about something.

Zeke glanced over at him. "Have you met any?"

"Two. A dominant bull and a calf that had gotten turned around."

Zeke waited, half expecting Ryker to be joking, but he continued. "Wild elk run in giant herds often split by gender. There's also a matriarchal leadership system similar to the panther clans, except with shifters the difference is the head is the male or bull. I don't know anything else except that they are nearly extinct. We have a small local herd that we try to watch out for, but they don't interact with us. I was just acknowledged once when we stopped a group of hunters from killing a calf that had been chased and got split from the herd." He looked at Red, who had turned around and was leaning against the wall with his arms crossed. "I can't honestly say that's what I smelled on Bodhi."

"Just shifter but not what?" Red queried and Zeke knew Red was confused that Ryker didn't know. Zeke didn't know how he could be expected to, though.

"He didn't smell like the bull."

"You were there?" Chrissy asked, and Red nodded.

"It was when we were scoping out this area for the rescue head-quarters. You'd gotten the chance to buy the land." He looked at Zeke, who nodded in apparent agreement.

Ryker glanced around. "That's it then. As soon as we hear I want Chrissy, Red, Zeke and Darriel with me. Fox, you secure the compound and get TJ to help you."


They all stood and Darriel noticed Zeke getting to his feet a lot more smoothly than he had yesterday.

Did he dare? "Zeke?"

Zeke turned immediately as everyone else filed out. Ryker shut the door behind him, leaving the two of them in the room.

"Can we talk?" Darriel half expected Zeke to shoot him down like he had done to him yesterday. And he wouldn't blame him. Zeke nodded warily. Darriel sat down and Zeke took the chair next to him.

"I'm not brave," Darriel started and held his hand up when Zeke opened his mouth. "Please," he whispered. He would only have the courage to do this once. Zeke nodded but kept silent. "I have some questions and I will only ask them once, then not ever bother you again."

Zeke swallowed and almost absentmindedly Darriel watched the lump travel down Zeke's throat. Then he met his big, beautiful eyes and suddenly he had courage. "I felt that you were interested in me originally. I know it started as kindness and friendship, but on my side, certainly, it grew into something more." Zeke's eyes widened but he stayed silent.

"If you don't feel the same, I understand. I'm only asking because I don't want there to be any misunderstandings. Like if you're not interested because I'm an omega or because I'm younger." He curled his fingers into fists to stop them from trembling. "Or that you're not bi or that I could never hope to replace Josie." And then Darriel couldn't talk anymore. Not because he lacked courage, *but because Zeke was kissing him.*

It took Darriel a second to realize he hadn't conjured up some fantasy when Zeke lightly nipped his bottom lip to shock him back into the moment. Then Darriel was kissing him back. He wrapped his arms around the back of Zeke's neck and clung on as Zeke dragged him from the chair and onto his lap. He had a brief worry he might hurt him, but then the next onslaught of lips and tongue and teeth shut down all those thoughts and Darriel melted into a physical touch he'd never known before.

He'd never been kissed, but instinctively he knew this wasn't some precursor to another stage, it was an alpha's stamp of ownership. Human or not, Darriel recognized Zeke's possession when he felt it and it thrilled him. Zeke couldn't have answered his question more loudly if he had shouted from the rooftops. Zeke threaded his fingers through Darriel's hair and used it to move his head to a better angle for him, breaking off and kissing and biting up his throat. Darriel felt each mark simultaneously in his groin and tried—desperately tried—for friction. Anything to relieve the uncomfortable pressure against his zipper.

"Zeke," Darriel murmured. "Please." Zeke stopped and rested his head against Darriel's neck. "I just meant not here," he rushed out in case Zeke misunderstood. Zeke leaned back and brushed Darriel's hair over his shoulder.

"You are too damn pretty."

Darriel was helpless to stop the pleased smile. "You make me feel pretty." He shook his head in wonder. *Was this really happening?* Zeke shuffled Darriel to his feet. He stood up next to him.

"Let's go check on the girls, then we can go find somewhere more private to talk."

Darriel nodded and obediently followed him out of the room, nerves all crowding back into his belly because Zeke hadn't used talk as a euphemism. It sounded more serious than that and even though Zeke had kissed him, Darriel wasn't a hundred percent sure he was going to like what he was going to say.

# Chapter Seven

I *should be stronger than this.* But Zeke hadn't counted on Darriel's strength or his body suddenly flaring back to life when he was least expecting it. He had been controlled and disciplined for so long that the desperate need to touch, to kiss Darriel, had overtaken him so suddenly he had reacted before his brain had kicked in.

Fox pushed himself off the wall as soon as they walked out. Zeke forced himself to meet his eyes even as Darriel slid a little behind him. "Charles and Kai have taken the kids for a walk out front. Emmy and Karina are with them. Charles said either join them or take the time to have a rest. He'd like the kids to interact a little if you're okay with it, like them to spend some time together. They're watched, safe, and Dinah is with them too."

Zeke was impressed. He wasn't sure he'd ever heard Fox say so much in one go before, but he glanced at Darriel. This had to be his decision.

"He's sure?" Darriel chewed his lip and Zeke had to nearly physically restrain himself from using his fingers to ease Darriel's abused flesh away from his teeth.

Fox nodded. "I might go see if they need a hand as well." With that he turned and walked toward the kitchen.

Zeke glanced at Darriel, his eyebrow raised. "My room in case they need anything for the girls?" Because he had no intention of anyone interrupting them. Darriel nodded and Zeke took his hand. Darriel's room was on the omega side, as Ryker coined it. The room Zeke was in at the moment was near the medical center. The bigger permanent suites, such as Marco and Kai's, were on this side too. Even though Zeke felt guilty taking up one of the larger rooms, there was no way he could stay on the omega side. It wouldn't be fair to the traumatized omegas just getting used to having a safe space.

He opened his door and tried to see it from Darriel's eyes even though Darriel had been in there before. Very bare. Since Emmett had mated Ryker, he had stayed here more often. He had gradually added some clothes and toiletries so he could stay at the last minute. Lots of books because of Darriel, but nothing else.

He had every intention of taking Darriel to the corner where there were a couple of easy chairs, but the second he closed the door Darriel stepped up close to him and Zeke's hand cupped his cheek almost of its own accord. He stared at Darriel's sleek black hair, his smooth light brown skin, and his huge eyes that were so expressive. "You are beautiful."

Darriel's cheeks darkened. He closed his eyes, pressing his cheek into Zeke's palm. "You keep saying that."

Zeke chuckled. "Because it's true." He glanced at the chairs. "We should talk."

Darriel opened his eyes, worry flaring in them, and he straightened up. Zeke caught his arm before he stepped away. "I just want to say I don't understand how you could possibly find me attractive. I'm human and way too old for you."

"I'm human," Darriel whispered, but he straightened, and Zeke wrapped his arms around him.

"I mean not a shifter."

A spark of something almost like humor shone in Darriel's eyes. "Technically, neither am I."

Which made Zeke's lips twitch. "You're twenty years younger than I am."

"I know. And?"

"And I will be old..."

"You do know you will age considerably slower if we bond?"

"But you won't ever catch up," Zeke said in frustration. "What if the day comes that you're sick of being with an old man?"

"What if I had died before Seth and Jesse got to me?"

Zeke hissed in a breath and clutched Darriel to him. He couldn't even speak his fear. They stood for a moment before Zeke felt the pull on his back and eased his hold.

"And speaking of Seth and Jesse," Darriel continued. "Did you know Seth is a human whereas Jesse is a bear shifter and there are twenty years between them?"

"Seventeen," Zeke croaked out, "which is considerably less than twenty-three."

"And shifters live up to around one hundred and twenty. But like I said, I could have died."

Zeke kissed into Darriel's hair. "Live for today you mean?"

"And I think with the girls we have enough babies."

Zeke huffed out a laugh. He knew human men didn't have the gene required to enable a male shifter pregnancy. Or not a gene exactly, something to do with the pH of the sperm. The scientists he had employed had explained their reasonings, but it was why Seth would never be able to get Jesse pregnant. It never once explained why Jesse got pregnant though. Neither of them seemed to mind, though, from what he could see.

Max, the bear shifter brother of May, was in charge of the lab. He had outsourced things to many different labs so no single human would be able to know too much. But Max knew a considerable amount about shifter health and since Zeke had found Emmett, all their resources were now going into research on male pregnancy. He knew the shifter birth rate was very low and that omega births were high risk and their babies often small. There was a very small window between the babies being fully formed and able to breathe on their own and them being delivered. Sometimes too small.

"We can go sit over there if you would rather."

Zeke groaned. He had a gorgeous man waiting in his arms willing to be kissed, and Zeke was busy thinking about the pH of sperm. "I'm sorry. You distracted me with talking about Seth and Jesse."

"In a good way?"

Zeke took in Darriel's anxious expression—the worry lines around his eyes and the slight tremble of his lips—and realized how much damned courage it had taken for Darriel to talk to him. "You are amazing." He kissed his lips but pulled back. "I know in your world attraction is instant. In my world, while that sometimes happens, I like that we became friends first. If—If you really don't care—"

Darriel made some sort of impatient whine in the back of his throat and slammed his mouth onto Zeke's. Zeke immediately responded, taking over the kiss. Sucking and licking, pushing his tongue inside Darriel's mouth. He felt Darriel sag against him in surrender.

"Too many clothes," Zeke decreed and stripped Darriel, making sure he met his eyes. Darriel was gorgeous and he wanted the man to know how fucking irresistible he was. They toppled onto the bed, Zeke ignoring the occasional twinge from his sore skin, almost reveling in the fact that he could feel at all when he had come so close to not feeling anything ever again.

He knew shifters couldn't get human diseases, so he didn't bother with the assurances he might have with a new partner. Not that there had been many of them and he'd used condoms anyway. He'd never had that level of trust with anyone since Josie.

He loved Darriel's body. A mixture of sleek muscles and smooth skin. Hot, eager mouth and whispered words that were a delight. Darriel talked. As if suddenly given permission, he told in breathless gasps where he like Zeke's hands, to hold him harder, to move just an inch higher, to mark him. He wanted marking. It was as if he needed it and something primitive in Zeke responded. Every bite that drew blood, Darriel arched into. His cock was rock-hard and leaking copiously. Zeke reached under him and swirled the omega slick around Darriel's puckered hole while fastening his lips over Darriel's left nipple. The cry was instant and Darriel pumped semen into Zeke's hand. Zeke smiled to himself. *Good.* That meant he could slow things down, show Darriel how an alpha really should take care of him.

He waited until Darriel's eyes had opened, then held up his hand. Without hesitation, Darriel took hold and licked him clean. Zeke struggled to contain his groans. Every pass of that wicked tongue, he imagined it somewhere else, until he shuffled down and took Darriel's softening cock into his mouth. Darriel cried out again, but Zeke clasped each flailing hand and sucked and laved until Darriel was swelling once more under Zeke's tongue.

"Zeke," Darriel gasped, "I can't." But Zeke was confident he could, and he brought him to the brink over and over until Darriel was once more begging and arching into Zeke's touch. Then he gasped again, and Zeke swallowed the semen that flooded his mouth. With a final lick, he let go of Darriel's cock. Rearing up, he took Darriel's lips in a bruising, punishing kiss, then gentled until he had Darriel squirming and moaning underneath him. In the back of his mind, Zeke knew alpha wolves could get an omega to have multiple orgasms, and damned if he didn't want to prove the same. He lined himself up and pushed. The slick of Darriel's channel was indescribably good, and Zeke had to clamp down on everything not to simply explode there and then. He didn't have a knot, but he could make it as good. He pulled out—the glide easy—and Darriel groaned, his fingers digging into Zeke's shoulders, the sting from his nails utterly perfect. Zeke thrust back in and Darriel gasped. "Once more baby, you can do it."

"No," Darriel whispered unbelievingly.

"Yes," Zeke's voice rang out in command, and he bent down and bit Darriel's nipple. Darriel arched and cried out, more cum pumping between them, and Zeke responded by letting himself go. Heat seared Zeke's body. Every cell lit up, and fire ignited every nerve. For a moment Zeke was lost. Existing in a world solely made of pleasure and sensation, until he slammed back down to be held in an embrace even better than that.

He had just enough strength left to gather a limp and sated Darriel in his arms and promise the heavens he would never let him go.

Zeke woke first to a notification beep on his phone. He extricated himself from a sleeping Darriel and picked it up. It was from Emmett saying not to worry, that Emmy and Karina were fine, and to take all the time he needed. Emmett followed that with at least a dozen heart emojis and Zeke rolled his eyes.

"What is it?" Darriel sat up, panic in his voice, the sheet pooling around his waist.

"Nothing," Zeke passed him the phone and watched as a small smile crept over Darriel's face.

"I think," Zeke rolled his shoulders experimentally, feeling the odd twinge and pull from his healing scars and the bruises on his ribs. "We should grab a shower then some food."

Darriel's smile widened. "Tell me about your other job. The one that pays for the rescue."

"I can do much better than that," Zeke said. "How about in a couple of days we take the girls out, grab lunch in Asheville, and I'll show you the offices. You can meet May." Darriel froze and Zeke tried to work out what was wrong. "We don't have to."

"You want to take us out?" Darriel asked in awe.

Zeke gathered the younger man into his arms. "Of course, I do. We don't need to worry that either of the girls are going to shift suddenly, and I'd like to show you what else I do."

Then he remembered he couldn't take Darriel anywhere because it wasn't safe and a huge weight seemed to almost suffocate him. *What was he doing? How could he have forgotten?*

"Zeke?" Darriel whispered softly when Zeke had come to a complete standstill.

Zeke cupped his cheek. "As much as I'd like to get back in bed, I need something to eat and so do you." Zeke held his hand out to Darriel as he looked ruefully at the bed. "We need to grab a shower and change the sheets."

Zeke loved the fact that the showers—built for men Ryker's size—meant they could both get in together. He thoroughly soaped and rinsed Darriel's skin and if that meant he spent a little longer on certain areas until Darriel was moaning and quivering with need, well, no one was around to call him on it. He turned Darriel around and pulled him back against him, squirting shampoo into his long black hair.

Of course, by the time he had washed it, because of the amazing sounds dripping from Darriel's lips, Zeke was hard as well. Darriel turned and they met in a rush of tongues and lips, cocks sliding and rubbing together deliciously until Zeke took them both in his hand and finished them off. Darriel sagged against him, and Zeke smiled in satisfaction. He was conceited enough he supposed to love that Darriel trusted him to take his weight, shifter or no shifter, and he quickly rinsed them both. He got out first and grabbed a towel to tie around him, then two more. One to wrap around Darriel while he sat him down, and the other to dry his hair with.

"You're spoiling me," Darriel murmured, eyes closed as Zeke gently dried his hair.

"You deserve spoiling." Zeke brushed his lips over Darriel's before seeing to himself. "Do you mind borrowing some clothes?" He wasn't about to let Darriel walk to the kitchen in a robe.

Darriel shook his head shyly and let Zeke pick some out for him. They were similar in height even if Darriel was slenderer. Once dressed, Zeke opened the door and steered Darriel to the kitchen. It was remarkably quiet, thank goodness. Isabelle was stirring something that smelled amazing, and Zeke's belly growled.

She chuckled. "I have some chicken and dumplings keeping warm or there's beef sandwiches in the fridge. This chili will be ready in a few minutes and the biscuits are about done as well."

Zeke might have whimpered...a little. He glanced at Darriel.

"Chicken, please," Darriel answered promptly.

Isabelle waved her spoon at the tables. "Go sit yourselves down and I'll bring it over."

"I can—" But Isabelle almost glared at Zeke.

"My son—our whole family—is safe and happy because of you. Go sit down."

"Yes, ma'am," Zeke responded and did as he was told. He knew every rescue took a team, but she clearly wanted to express her thanks.

Darriel took him to the table in the corner and after a moment Zeke realized it had a good view of the front yard. In the distance they could see the group of kids with Charles and Emmett. They were all bundled up but racing around happily in the fallen leaves. Darriel smiled and turned back. "I think you have a fan."

Zeke squirmed a little. "I'm one of a team, and it's not like I actually do the rescuing." He certainly didn't expect her to wait on him.

"They were frantic about Teo."

"Their youngest?"

Darriel nodded. "They have three. Aldred and Rhys can both shift, but Teo's an omega. I wish I was a bear," he added after a moment.

"Because bear omegas can shift," Zeke said in understanding, knowing Jesse could. Isabelle arrived with their food and Zeke thanked her. She made them promise to just ask if they wanted anything else and they both tucked into the meal. Zeke managed nearly all of his, but Darriel was pushing his around after only a few mouthfuls.

"Not hungry?"

Darriel shrugged. "I got used to eating less."

Zeke sat back a little and patted his knee. "Come here."

Darriel looked up startled but moved. "I'm too heavy," he protested as Zeke scoffed and sat him on his lap. Zeke picked up a piece of chicken and offered it. Darriel obediently opened his mouth and chewed. Zeke didn't want to force him if he wasn't hungry, but he had an idea that there was something else going on here. He knew omegas were naturally slim, but Darriel was almost gaunt and having a shifter metabolism even if his animal was dormant meant he needed extra calories.

"Being with me is a double-edged sword."

Darriel paused but then opened his lips for the next morsel Zeke passed him. He chewed and swallowed. "You mean because you're not a shifter?"

Zeke grinned. He imagined his smile could be called wicked. "Nope." He swallowed a piece of chicken, then offered Darriel another before he answered. "You should know—in case you hadn't already worked it out—I'm a domineering bastard. I'm in charge in any relationship. A dominant, if you like, for those into that sort of thing, but at its basic level if I think you're doing something detrimental to your health I will interfere." He looked Darriel right in the eye. "I want nothing more than to take care of my partner in every way. A lot of people find that smothering."

Darriel thought it sounded wonderful, but he didn't say that because he thought Zeke wasn't finished.

"For starters, I've been thinking about the school. Nema's fantastic, but we need to work out specialist teachers as well. What if one of the pups wants to learn to play the violin, for example?"

Darriel gaped. He didn't seem able to voice a reply even if he had one. Zeke was talking like he was going to be involved in the girls' future. His pulse quickened. This was really happening.

"Shifter society is good because it places importance on family bonds, but only when every member of that family fits in. The kids are taught to survive in a human world. I want them to *thrive.*

Secrecy has always been a huge thing, and while I approve, I don't think it's realistic to expect shifters to be a secret forever. I think we should make sure our children are prepared. How do we know Karina doesn't want to be an international concert pianist or to be the next scientist that makes a breakthrough in the fight against cancer? How do we know Emmy doesn't want to be a surgeon or a general in the army? She may want to be the best mother in the world, but that should be an and/or choice, not because she couldn't do anything else."

Darriel couldn't speak around the huge lump in his throat.

Zeke's voice softened. "Why shouldn't we have the same hopes and dreams for our children as every other set of parents has had since forever? We spend so much time and effort on not being found out that we forget to live."

Zeke brushed the wetness from under Darriel's eyes. "I get carried away. I say 'we', but I won't apologize because I've felt like one of you for a long time. Deep down I know if shifter society wasn't shrouded in so much secrecy Josie would be alive."

Darriel's heart skipped a beat. He couldn't compete with this and even though it killed him, he didn't want to. He tried to lean back, but Zeke's arms tightened.

"She was also a long time ago. I will never forget Josie or think of her without affection, but a certain omega wolf shifter has my attention and so much more. If he wants it, that is."

Darriel couldn't have spoken if his life depended on it.

"All I'm saying is, I'm not easy. I have a business away from here and for a million different reasons I can't give that up. Karina and Emmeline need me to never give that up." He pinned Darriel's gaze. "*You* need me to never give that up."

Darriel knew that. Knew that if he stayed with Zeke his life—the girls' lives—would change. Could he do that? He was nothing. He had no skills.

"Whatever that thought was, stop it," Zeke chided. "You are the best person to fight for omega rights."

"What?" Darriel whispered, completely aghast.

Zeke smoothed his hair and kissed his lips. "I'm not suggesting tomorrow. I'm not suggesting this year, but it's coming. It might be twenty years away, but our kids need to be taught to be proud of who they are, not to constantly hide it."

He was right. Darriel knew it. He didn't know if he could step up, but at some point, someone would have to.

They spent the rest of the day simply hanging out with the girls and when evening came around, much as he hated it, sleeping apart from Zeke tonight was the right thing to do. He wanted nothing more than to spend the night in his arms, but he had some thinking to do. Ryker told them they were meeting the Davies brothers mid-morning. Darriel knew Zeke didn't like him going, but if he was going to be brave enough to be a part of the future Zeke thought was coming, then he needed to do this.

He actually slept better than he was expecting to until around five thirty when Emmy decided she was starving and needed attention. Right. Now. There was a soft knock at the door and Darriel's heart jumped. Was it Zeke? He opened it and Charles smiled at him, then beamed at Emmy. "I was just on my way back from the kitchen with some milk for Maisie. I just took it in there and came back because I could hear her. Do you need any help?"

Darriel smiled in gratitude. Charles took that as a yes and had Emmy changed and her bottle ready in no time. Charles smiled. "You seem happier."

Darriel chuckled at the obvious curiosity. "I think you were right. We talked." *And did a lot of other things.*

"Must have been one hell of a conversation to put that look on your face."

Darriel could feel his face heat, but he smiled. "Maybe."

Charles's grin widened when there was another knock at the door and Blue put his head around the door.

"I'm sorry, but I'm not on my own."

Charles glanced at Darriel. "We've been having a few issues. Who's with you?"

Blue winced. "Daniel, Mo and Maisie. Raine and Kelly are staying with Vinny."

Darriel chuckled, he couldn't help it. Feeling inexplicably lighter, he beckoned them in. Blue led in three of the kids from the Columbia pack. Blue, who was nine, had come from the same pack but had immediately grown quite close to Charles, protective almost. Vinny was another new transfer. At thirteen, he wasn't thrilled with babysitting duty, but he knew if he wanted separate time to play video games uninterrupted, that was the price he had to pay. It worked.

The last child, Luca, had basically adopted Kai and Marco as his new family and was with them. The fact that Charles was so good with the remaining kids meant there wasn't any resentment, or none past the usual childhood squabbles anyway.

"Is that Emmy?" Maisie piped up, coming to stand next to Charles and pressing into his side. The other two crowded around.

"This is Emmy," Charles agreed, "you saw her on our walk."

"She's really little," Maisie pronounced.

"That's because she's only seven weeks old."

"And this is Karina," Darriel said. "She's Emmy's sister."

Mo turned, silent as usual, and fixed big eyes on Darriel. Darriel's heart melted. Neither Mo nor Daniel had talked for a long time since they arrived, but he'd heard Daniel talk since. He knew Charles was concerned that Mo still wasn't talking and hoped Marco's contact would be able to help. "Do you want to say hello?"

Blue held his hand out for Mo, and Mo took it. They walked over and Darriel smiled. "If you sit in the chair, you can hold her."

Mo looked at Blue as if needing confirmation, but Darriel stood, and Blue helped Mo climb on the chair. Darriel snagged a pillow from the bed and laid it across Mo's tiny knees, then showed him where to put his arms and laid Karina in them. Karina had finished her milk but hadn't been in quite so much of a hurry to go back to sleep. If it had been Emmy, she'd have been fussing since, unless the little madam was asleep, she didn't do "still." Karina, however, was quiet. She looked up at Mo with apparent fascination. Mo was simply awed. He gazed at Karina then Blue. Karina blew bubbles and waved her hand. Very slowly, Mo touched the tip of one of his fingers to her little fist, and quick as anything, she curled her fingers around it. Mo's lips parted in utter astonishment, then he glanced up, a smile curling his lips. Darriel could have kissed his daughter. He didn't know exactly what had happened to the kids, but having their home and their family ripped apart was bad enough.

Of course, then Maisie wanted a turn. Daniel was more interested in the squishy toys in the corner and happily amused himself. After a few minutes, Charles got up and laid a sleeping Emmy in the stroller and put a finger to his lips. "We have to be quiet so we don't wake her."

Darriel took Karina from Maisie, who jumped down and took the hand Blue held out. Darriel watched as they all trooped out for breakfast and wondered about what Zeke had said. There were a lot of kids who deserved a chance to thrive.

# Chapter Eight

Zeke didn't like this one bit.

As Ryker drove, he sat in the truck with Red, Chrissy, and Darriel on their way to meet the Davies brothers. They had gone back and forth on tactics for most of the morning. Since the meeting place was out in the open, they couldn't have any close backup, but it also meant neither could the Davies brothers. He didn't like the whole set up, and that Darriel was here, even less. They were only here because of Bodhi. The fact was, they didn't even know if he would be there, or if Bobby and Bodhi were even the same person. Concerning the property, he knew legally the brothers didn't have a leg to stand on.

"Have you made any decisions about your new gammas?" Zeke wanted to distract himself and knew Ryker was thinking about adding more pack members. They needed more security with the number of omegas and kids increasing.

"Sam seems to be working out, but he's more interested in working with Marco than pulling gate duty." Zeke didn't blame him.

"Did I see TJ the other day?" He barely remembered being dropped off, just the giddy relief and the pain he'd been in.

Ryker nodded. "He wanted to stay with the rangers, but he lost his job."

"Why?" Zeke was shocked. TJ was a reliable member of Rescue One.

"Family problems. Ginny's dad is human, and he's got dementia. Between him and the fact that they've got three pups under five and another on the way, he missed a lot of work."

"Let me know if he needs extra help."

"It's covered, but thanks." They both heard the Davies brothers' pickup trundle into the field barely ten seconds after them. Zeke couldn't tell if Bodhi was in there at this distance. Ryker pulled up and turned to look at Darriel. "Unless you see Bodhi, stay in the truck."

Porter got out of the driver's side, immediately followed by Paxton on the passenger's side. Porter had his shotgun, but this time so did Red. Wolves didn't usually carry guns and Ryker hated them, but as he'd explained to Zeke, he wasn't risking them looking defenseless. Zeke had his own gun, but it was secured in the gun safe at his office. He hadn't even wanted it in the safe back at the apartment while Trina was there.

They all walked cautiously toward each other. Zeke had decided to act like the business partner he was. He'd even dressed the part. In fact, he'd enjoyed the reaction from Darriel this morning when he'd seen him in the suit. It was damn cold and while Zeke saw Ryker had jeans and a T-shirt on—shifter metabolism—he'd added his dark wool overcoat. He'd also insisted that Darriel borrow one of Emmett's jackets and made a mental note to get him and the girls a winter wardrobe asap.

He knew as soon as he was out of the car that he had the brothers' focus and decided to roll with it. "I understand you are disputing our rightful purchase of your deceased father's land. I'm not sure why, therefore, you would want to meet outside my attorney's office or indeed why you would want to meet at all."

Paxton stepped in front of his brother and scoffed, then turned to

Ryker. "Because what we have to tell you is for your ears only." he smirked. "We heard you had a bit of a problem with wild animals, so to speak."

By not so much as one muscle did Ryker's face change, even though Zeke and everyone else knew exactly what Paxton was implying. Suspicion and fact didn't always go hand in hand though. Did they know? Zeke would have dismissed it completely if Darriel hadn't said he had seen Porter turn up on shifter land unchallenged.

"Zeke Coleman is my business partner," Ryker said mildly, deliberately ignoring the taunt.

Porter sneered but turned to the truck and beckoned. Zeke's heart started beating faster as the door opened and the young man he'd seen a picture of got out. At the same time, he heard a truck door open behind him and knew Darriel had seen the man and was joining them. Paxton flicked a gaze over to Darriel, but he didn't show any signs of recognition. Neither did Porter. Darriel simply came and stood behind Ryker and Zeke.

Then the young man looked up and Red swore. The injuries to his face were appalling. He had a fresh black eye, a split lip, bruises covering his chin and throat, what looked like a broken cheekbone, and he was limping. Red snarled and took a step forward. The boy yelped and took a step behind Porter. Porter laughed. Red came to an immediate stop, the incredulity as he turned to Ryker clear. Zeke narrowed his eyes. For some unknown reason, it was clear that the young man was more frightened of shifters than he was of the two assholes who had hurt him. It made no sense.

"Well, now we're all here," Paxton continued. "This is how it's gonna be. You sign the deed gifting me back my Pop's land and we'll keep quiet about what Bobby here has told us. Not that we needed much confirmation, you understand. I believe you knew an old business buddy of mine, name of Riggs. Porter here met him so many times his muscle assumed he was to go unchallenged. It was interesting what he saw the time they weren't expecting him to turn up."

He flicked an eye over Bobby. "And my nephew here was willing to tell us all sorts of things. Things I'm sure the papers would pay a lot of money to get their hands on."

"And just in case you're willing to risk further accidental damage to the boy—" Porter chimed in and glanced at his brother. "Should I say cub? Puppy, maybe?" Porter grinned, clearly enjoying himself, and flicked a glance at Red, who didn't seem able to stop the warning rumble. He jerked a chin at his brother. "Someone needs a leash."

Ryker took a step closer to Red, clearly concerned. Zeke knew the brothers were dumb, but baiting Red was going to be suicidal if they weren't careful. The trouble was, other people could get caught in the crosshairs. He wished Darriel would get back in the truck.

"The evidence is with a friend," Porter continued. "He so much as smells anything happened to either of us, he goes to the papers."

"But, so you know we're reasonable, we'll give you a few days to think about it." Paxton eyed Bobby. "But don't take too long. As you can see, the boy's real clumsy. Don't know how he might get hurt if we get too distracted worrying about the land you stole to watch over him properly."

Darriel made a low sound in the back of his throat and Bobby seemed to notice him for the first time. Even Zeke could see the surprise and recognition that flickered in the young man's eyes. They had their confirmation without Darriel needing to say one word.

Zeke nodded as if that was a perfectly reasonable explanation and took a small step forward, drawing both the brothers' attention. "We can give you an answer very soon, but you should also realize one thing. Speculative and clearly ridiculous stories can be hushed up for those who have limitless funds to pay for it. In case you don't know who I am, my name is Zeke Coleman and I own Coleman Investments, among other things. I suggest you google it when you get home. You should also know that my friends here are all volatile and quick to anger—a little like wild animals, shall we say, seeing as how you want to use that sort of comparison." He nodded over to Red who looked like he was ready to rip them to shreds. "If you were dead, it wouldn't matter how much land you were gifted, would it?"

Paxton opened his mouth, but Zeke didn't give him the chance to respond.

"So, when we meet next, if I see so much as a fresh broken fingernail on that boy's body, all bets, and all *leashes*, are very much off."

Paxton grunted, then jerked his head back toward the truck. Porter got in and started the engine. Bodhi took one sorrowful look at Darriel, dropped his gaze, turned and followed Paxton into the pickup. They all stood and watched as the pickup bounced down the hill.

Zeke put his arm around Darriel as he pressed into him, obviously seeking comfort. Red made a completely disgusted noise, tossed his gun at Chrissy, turned and ran. All they heard was the sound of tearing clothes as they watched a wolf run for the trees.

Zeke met Ryker's eyes. He knew. In his heart of hearts, he knew what he had to do, and he hated it with everything in him. Because the very thing that could actually get the shifter council to get off their asses and do something was the threat of discovery. And the one person who could help was the last person he wanted to ask. But he needed to warn them. "We'll go back and call Regina."

When they got back to the pack house, Zeke made Darriel promise to eat something as he left to join the other omegas and get Emmy and Karina. Ryker put the phone down as he walked into the smaller room he kept for meetings. "Has Red come back?"

Chrissy shook her head and looked at Ryker. "This seems more than just genuine concern."

Ryker huffed out a laugh. "They never even touched."

Zeke looked from one to the other. "What does that matter?"

"The only thing that would cause such an extreme reaction in a shifter, usually, is protecting their mate, but they never even touched. They never got closer than eight feet apart," Chrissy said. "Scent might have come into play, but in the middle of a field with gun oil and unwashed bodies?"

"It was the only benefit of meeting in a field I could see," Zeke agreed dryly.

"I just spoke to Regina. She'll be here in a couple of hours, but Marco just called to remind me Chris and his father are on their way to see Mo. Everyone's been warned. Emmett and Dinah are going to watch the rest of the kids so Charles can be with Mo." He eyed Zeke. "It might be good you're here."

Zeke's eyebrows rose questioningly.

"We've sold this place before as a residential retreat belonging to the charity. Abused spouses, etcetera. You being here visiting adds validity to that argument."

Zeke nodded. "What time will he be here?"

"On his way."

# Chapter Nine

In the end, the only thing that would get Mo to sit and let Griffin Deerman look at his throat was Karina. Zeke watched as Mo was charmed again by the little girl's calmness. Darriel had stayed with Emmy and actually let Zeke walk out holding Karina. She was awake and watching him with those huge brown eyes just like her daddy's, and he was amazed she wasn't picking up on his nerves.

Zeke had faced down a boardroom full of investors. Met and calmed angry shifters. Had people wave guns at him. Nothing had made him nervous like the thought of being a hundred percent responsible for a tiny human being. He'd even spent time with Josie quite confidently, but this seemed different somehow. Charles had come looking for them a few minutes ago to ask for Karina. Ryker wanted Zeke to meet the doctor, so he had suggested Zeke bring her.

Or Zeke thought that was why. Darriel's twinkling eyes as he handed her over might have said something else, but he had bravely taken her and followed Charles. He hadn't been in the large area Charles and the kids occupied before. There was one large room with sofas, bean bags, toys and a large TV. A couple of tables sat to one side where the kids could have snacks or do homework. One side had a small corridor leading to the bedrooms and they could now sleep ten in pairs. He noticed Blue coming out of one of the bedrooms and walking to the door, then he seemed to change his mind and sat on one of the benches. Zeke turned back as he heard Charles solemnly explain to Mo that the doctor had to look at Karina's throat as well, and because Karina trusted Mo, would he mind holding her while the doctor shined a little light in there?

Zeke was impressed with Griffin, as he had asked them to call him, or Dr. G. for the kids. He was around sixty, Zeke guessed, with an easygoing manner and wide smile that quickly calmed the kids.

Zeke arranged Karina on Mo's knee and stepped back to let Griffin and Charles do their thing. The flashlight experiment, first on the baby and then on Mo, went very smoothly. Then, of course, all the kids wanted the light shone in their throat and Griffin obliged. The older kids, except Blue, had all stayed out of the way, but Zeke knew Blue was Charles's unofficial assistant, so he wasn't surprised he was there. The little ones were in no danger of shifting and they were all very content to be the focus of someone new. Darriel knew Charles was relieved. According to Blue, there were at least three pregnant omegas but none of the ones left alive after the shootout had claimed these five kids. Despite the fact that the new alpha wanted to keep them, since they'd used guns and that had involved the human sheriffs, the council had quietly removed them before the humans even knew they were there.

Dinah served Dr. G coffee and cake when he was done, and the kids went off to play in the corner while Ryker and Charles discussed Mo. Zeke sat with Karina and listened.

"I can't find any obvious injuries," Griffin said thoughtfully. "You said he has no medical history?"

Ryker shook his head. "As Chris explained, a lot of these kids were born 'off the grid'. We are doing what we can, but it's a long process." Zeke knew most shifter births were "off the grid." He didn't know if Darriel had a birth certificate or a social security number. He knew Emmett did and so did Josie. He'd also bet neither of the girls' births were registered and mentally added it to his list. He looked down as Karina's eyes started to close and pressed a gentle kiss on her forehead. He inhaled the baby smell that reminded him of her daddy.

"Usually, I would say further medical investigation was in order, but I can see in the short term, taking the little boy anywhere would be traumatic," Griffin said thoughtfully. "I know quite a few child psychologists I could recommend."

Zeke saw the look Ryker sent Charles and understood the difficulties. Then he noticed Kelly sidling up to them.

"Hi, sweetie, do you want some juice?" Charles stood ready to go get her some, but she shook her head and turned to the doctor.

"Blue's sick."

Griffin frowned. "Blue?"

Zeke looked over to the small area where the tables were, just as Ryker stood up. Blue still sat at one of them, shoulders hunched, his head in his hands. Vinny sat next to him talking quietly.

Charles stood. "I'll go and see—"

"Nonsense," Griffin said and stood. "Lead on." He held his hand out and Kelly took it, leading him solemnly across the room. Vinny looked up, shot to his feet and sent a desperate glance to Ryker, and Ryker moved very quickly to get to Blue first.

Vinny turned and said, "He's just caught a cold. Everything's fine."

Zeke had a moment of confusion because shifters didn't get colds. He glanced at Charles. What was wrong?

"Nonsense. Colds can be miserable things." Griffin stepped up to Blue and Vinny blocked him. Ryker hunched down and started talking to him in gentle tones.

"I really think," Griffin started sounding annoyed, but just at that second Blue looked up and snarled. The noise that came from his throat wasn't anything a human could make.

Griffin gaped and took a step back. "What on earth?"

Zeke swore silently. Blue was going into his first shift, right there in front of the doctor.

"Griffin," Charles said trying to distract him. "Perhaps—"

But it was too late, with another growl Blue shuddered and Zeke had a second to see hair sprout all over the boy's body. Griffin staggered back as a bobcat stood and shook out its fur. For a full second no one said a thing, then Ryker bent down to the trembling cat and murmured soothing words, pulling torn clothing off him. "Come with me," he encouraged, then unbuttoned his shirt. He sent a fatalistic look at Zeke, shrugged down his pants, and shifted. Zeke glanced in concern at Griffin, who had gone gray.

"Shall we sit down?" he suggested, and steered the doctor to a seat. Zeke didn't know what must be worse. Seeing humans turn into animals or the fact that the other kids were completely unconcerned. Kelly lunged for Blue before anyone could stop her and flung her arms around the animal's neck.

"Yes," she giggled. "A kitty," and looked at Charles in excitement. Ryker nudged Kelly and she let Blue go. Then Ryker and Blue headed to the door. Vinny rushed over and opened it so they could leave, then looked at the kids.

"Let's go see if Dinah has cookies?" A cheer went up and they all followed him out.

The silence seemed to stretch endlessly to the far corners of the room. Charles got Griffin a glass of water and pushed it over to him after he sat down. He shot Zeke a pleading look and Zeke nodded once, accepting the responsibility. "Do you want to take Karina to Darriel and go make sure everyone's okay?" Charles took her, nodded, and scooted out.

Griffin watched Charles go then turned to Zeke. "What the hell did you put in that coffee?"

Zeke grinned. "That was my reaction the first time I saw it as well."

"I don't know what question to ask first. Was it real?" Griffin took a sip of the water. "Did I really just see a young boy turn into a bobcat? And *Ryker*? He's a..."

"Wolf shifter," Zeke answered.

Griffin gulped and focused. "Can you?"

"Nope," Zeke grinned. "I'm just human. And now you know why a lot of the kids are born 'off-grid', but I'm trying to alter that."

"Chris, my son," Griffin suddenly asked. "Does he know?"

Zeke nodded. "We have a network of trusted humans who keep our secrets. He worked with one of the park ranger medics that's also one of us."

*"Marco?"*

Zeke nodded. "Can we trust you? Your son seemed to think so." Griffin waved a hand like he wanted more information, but then he paused.

"The little boy? Is he going to be a cat?" Zeke looked pointedly at him and raised his eyebrow. He needed a promise first. Griffin sighed. "Yes, of course. Provided," he added, "that the reason Mo isn't talking has nothing to do with trauma he might have suffered here."

So, Zeke explained what had happened to the kids and what Shifter Rescue did. Dinah came in later with more coffee and Griffin eyed her speculatively as she left.

"Yes," Zeke confirmed. "The only ones we don't know about for sure are the kids. They come from shifter parents, or one shifter and one regular human, but not all can shift."

"Really?" Griffin responded, and Zeke could see genuine curiosity mixed with a little excitement now that the man was recovering from his shock.

"I have a colleague who works in my research facility trying to find out why that is. I'd be happy to introduce the two of you."

"If this is as large as you say, how come there are no wolf doctors?" Griffin asked then huffed. "Veterinarians?"

Zeke told him about the challenges they faced and why most shifters stayed in heavily private communities. "That was a first shift. Blue is nine and first shifts often happen around that age, sometimes older. They're not generally so dramatic though, as I understand. They're often preceded by mild flu-like symptoms and the pup or cub has some warning. Blue's a good kid. This must have happened suddenly. Ryker took him out because Ryker's the alpha."

"Like the leader?" Griffin queried.

"Yes, but he's like a father to them as well. Shifters are very pack-orientated." He paused as his own words sank in. *Pack orientated.* He'd had an idea of building Darriel a house in Asheville for them, close enough for visits, but he couldn't do that. He mentally cursed at his own stupidity. How could they live here, and he still run the business? He focused back on the task at hand and answered Griffin's question.

"We don't have a doctor. Shifters don't get human illnesses. Our problems only arise with the children."

"But how does it *work*, the change?" Griffin asked in amazement. "The regeneration needed at a cellular level would be astonishing."

And that wasn't even the most surprising thing. He wasn't going to mention omegas though. That had to be Ryker's call. Men having babies might just be a bit too much for Griffin to handle at the moment.

"I would be very interested to meet your colleague," Griffin said thoughtfully. "I would also like to properly examine the children, but I think that needs to be scheduled over a period of time to get them used to me first." Zeke smiled in satisfaction. Griffin wasn't running for the hills. He'd been shocked obviously, but he was responding perfectly.

"We really could do with your help."

"Dad." They both turned. Zeke gathered that the young man who stood next to Marco was Griffin's son. It had been a damned good idea of whoever's to call him. "Are you okay?"

Griffin snorted and stood up. "I'm fine. Well, nothing that a shot of brandy won't cure. For medicinal purposes, obviously," Griffin added with a wink. Chris hugged his dad.

"I'm sorry I couldn't tell you, but they're good people."

Griffin returned the hug. "Chris, I understand patient confidentiality. Besides, I hate golf," he added cryptically.

Chris grinned and mock-punched his dad. "At least you won't be bored."

Marco stepped up. "Good to meet you again, sir." They shook hands.

"The kids are calling me Dr. G, but you can call me Griffin." He eyed Marco speculatively. "I'm assuming it was your idea to ask Chris to bring me here?" Zeke listened as they started talking about Mo and the possible tests he could do here.

"I have a small clinic if you'd like to see it?"

Griffin nodded to Marco enthusiastically and Zeke followed them out. As they walked into the kitchen, he immediately focused on Darriel holding Emmy and smiled. The answering smile he got in return gave him other ideas. But at that moment a car pulled up and he absently noted Regina had bought a newer model Mercedes. One he had been considering, although he would have to do some research on safety ratings and child restraints and... Zeke smiled a satisfied smile even as he watched the woman he didn't particularly care for exit the car as one of her claw held the door open for her. Marco hesitated at seeing her and glanced back at Zeke, obviously unsure of what to do. Zeke knew if Ryker was here, he would go outside to meet her and then escort her to the office. Zeke wasn't inclined to do that, but seeing as how she was here to help...

*Get yourself together,* Zeke scolded himself. He went to the door, but Emmett beat him to it. She smiled and walked toward her grandson, elegant as usual in her suit and three-inch heels. Zeke knew the pumps were Manolo Blahnik because May wore them.

"Who's that?" Zeke turned to see Griffin standing next to him.

"My son's grandmother," Zeke responded mildly.

Griffin seemed be in awe. "*My* grandmother never looked like that." Then they were inside, and introductions were made. Regina put out a hand to shake the doctor's, clearly knowing he was human, but he caught it, kissed it, and bowed theatrically. Chris rolled his eyes at Marco, but Regina merely smiled.

"It's nice to meet you, Dr. Deerman."

"Griffin, please."

Marco coughed politely to get the doc's attention and Regina turned to Zeke. "Zeke."

"Regina," he acknowledged, and then cursed to himself. Ryker was usually the barrier between them, and he wasn't here. He didn't know if Red was back and if what Chrissy said was true, it might not be a good idea to have him there anyway.

"Shall we go and talk?" He shot a soft smile to Darriel, then turned and escorted her to Ryker's office.

Magically, a tray of coffee had appeared. Regina declined Zeke's offer to prepare her a cup and merely helped herself, which surprised him. She stood next to him just adding cream while he doctored his own, and hesitated for a moment, the jug balanced in her fingers. Zeke was just going to ask if she preferred tea when she tilted her head as if she could hear something, but she didn't comment and took a seat.

"We just had a first shift right in front of the doctor. He's Chris Deerman's father from the ranger service. Chris used to work with Marco. I just added him to the list of trusted humans." Then he told her about Mo. "It will be beneficial having a doctor here, especially a pediatrician for the non-shifters." He felt like he had to justify himself, which he didn't.

Regina put her cup down. "I agree. Now, tell me about your mate. I'm assuming it's the delightful boy with the twins?"

It wasn't often that people surprised him, but the Panthera had done just that. He met her gaze and she smiled. "A Panthera's scenting abilities are similar to an alpha's." She shrugged. "But you know that." They were both silent for a few long seconds, each, he was sure, thinking of the same person. She glanced out of the window and for the first time in her presence Zeke felt a tug on his insides. Almost like they were sharing something.

"One of the reasons Josephine didn't want to be the Panthera was because she had such a gentle spirit. She'd been there when I had to discipline a member of the claw and it wasn't pretty."

"What happened?" Zeke didn't know which one of them was more surprised by the question. He'd never asked Regina anything before, he'd been too busy resenting her.

"Argyle was a bully. I inherited him from my mother, and I should have been strong enough to get rid of him earlier, but I was still feeling out my role and I thought I had bigger battles." She met his gaze. "I inherited the job at twenty-two. Both my parents died in a helicopter crash."

Zeke was stunned. He hadn't known that. Damn, that was young.

"Anyway, Argyle had certain sexual preferences involving minors. Apparently, it had been going on a long time, but this time the boy couldn't be bought. Argyle beat him to death and expected the clan to cover it up." She speared Zeke with her brilliant gaze. "Whatever you think of me, I don't condone rape or the actions of pedophiles."

"But you still covered it up."

"If by covering it up you mean killing Argyle instead of reporting him to the police, then I suppose I did. We didn't make a donation to the family because the reason the boy was homeless was his father tried the same thing and his mother didn't believe her son when he attempted to tell her. There is now a forty-bed shelter for vulnerable youth set up in Atlanta in his name. It's financially independent and will always be so, no matter what happens to me."

Zeke didn't know what to say. He had carried so many chips on his shoulder for so long he could build a wall with them. Even when he knew Regina hadn't actually ordered her daughter's death, he still blamed the clan system and ultimately her as head of it. *Because it's easier than blaming yourself,* a little voice whispered to him. Was that it? Had he fixated on Regina as a target because protecting Josie had been his responsibility and he hadn't been there?

"And I think we need to talk about your recent ordeal with the

Stanza clan, but I understand we have other issues, so let's start with the Davies brothers and the boy."

He was glad she wasn't pushing, even though he knew his head had been buried in the sand for far too long. His capture was like a sore spot in the back of his mind. It was Zeke's turn to look out of the window. What if Darriel wasn't the only thing keeping him here? It had quickly occurred to him that as easily as they had let him go, he could be recaptured. It caused a sick, heavy feeling in the pit of his stomach and he didn't know what to do about it. He'd pushed it to the back of his mind to deal with both Darriel and the Davies brothers, but he knew it wouldn't stay there forever. At some point he would have to face it. He couldn't live his life in fear. And he wouldn't be responsible for hurting Trina.

"Ryker says he can smell he's a shifter, but he can't identify what type. Darriel confirmed it's Bodhi, a child from the old Mills River omega house. As far as he was aware, the boy was a mixed breed, but he also doesn't know what type. We're meeting them again, supposedly to give in to their threat to out us to the press."

She hesitated.

"Ryker said there was a small Elk herd up the mountains. That they were insanely private. Do you think it's them?"

"No. Ryker would know; besides, he's met the bull and a calf."

The doubt must have registered on Zeke's face. Regina leaned forward. "What you have to realize is that as a powerful alpha, Ryker would know. The fact that he says Bodhi's a shifter but he doesn't know *what* worries me." She took a breath as if to say something, but her lips remained closed.

"What?" Zeke asked. Regina shook her head, but Zeke could tell there was something. He pushed. "No, what were you going to say?"

"I forgot there for a moment you're not a shifter." Zeke bristled. "Not for the reason you're thinking, but deep down we have a huge trust issue." Zeke nearly scoffed. She had that right. He knew she adored Emmett and Josie, but he still wasn't a hundred percent sure she would choose them over the clan.

"You misunderstand," Regina said dryly. "The issue is that I don't trust *you*. I'm past caring what you think of me."

Zeke opened his mouth to spew righteous denials but then what she said clicked. "You don't trust *me*?" What the fuck? He had kept their secrets for years!

"Ryker might, but I know you resent the clan for what happened to Josie. Plus, you were just treated to a nearly two-week fun stay with another clan. I don't trust you because I know you hate panthers."

Which was reasonable, for fuck's sake. If he'd been Regina, he wouldn't trust him either. "But I would never put this pack in jeopardy. Emmett. Ryker." *Darriel.*

She sighed. "I wish Ryker was here."

*So do I.* "I don't think he'll be long," Zeke said a little optimistically. Regina chuckled. It was the first amusement he had seen on her face since she had arrived.

"Ryker isn't just battling shifter dynamics, he's dealing with adolescent hormones," And Zeke felt himself smile. The shared humor when they never voluntarily shared anything else was startling.

"I would never betray this pack." It needed saying. "And, however I feel about our history, I love my son with every breath in my body and he loves you." Regina looked like she was going to say something, but he carried on. "I'm scared." He huffed, incredulous that he could admit that in front of this woman. "I'm scared that they won't come for me this time but instead for someone I love."

The release, the sheer relief at admitting, *acknowledging*, what was wrong made him giddy.

Regina's smile was understanding. "We are of the same mind." Then she completely stunned him. "Have you read The Jungle Book?"

It took Zeke a minute. "You mean the children's one?"

She shot him a quelling look. "Rudyard Kipling's is actually based on a true story and while humans credit it on an actual man found living with wolves in 1867 the real story is one of shifter legend and much older. According to shifter mythology Bagheera was a panther shifter."

Zeke might have gaped, but then he clarified. "*Mythology?* So you don't actually know?"

"Neither do the millions who believe in Christianity, Zeke. It's still what they believe." He inclined his head in acceptance.

"But this is going to be a little harder to swallow," she added with a tiny smirk. "It wasn't just the black panther—Bagheera—that was a shifter. Their greatest enemy was as well." Zeke had an awful thought about a snake and happily imagined Paxton Davies as one, then he thought about what Regina was really trying to tell him. It was incredible, unbelievable. He gazed at her.

"You mean *Shere Khan.*" Speechless didn't even cover this. She didn't need to vocalize agreement. Her expression said it all. "But I understood tiger shifters were extinct in the US."

"They are," she confirmed.

Zeke leaned back. "Then?"

Regina sighed. "Two things then. One fact, one rumor."

Zeke nodded.

"Ryker is a powerful alpha. He leads on instinct. It is totally inconceivable he wouldn't be able to place the shifter scent."

"But why, if he'd never come across it before?"

"Instinct. He would know."

"But the fact he doesn't blows that theory up."

Regina shook her head. "Not if the shifter can mask it."

"But you can do that." He seemed to be starting every sentence with "but".

"No, panthers don't mask their shifter scent. They simply don't have one."

Zeke turned at the sound of Ryker's voice. Regina didn't, which told him she knew he had been standing there. Made sense. "Meaning?" Zeke pushed.

Ryker pushed away from the doorway and eyed Regina. "That's what you genuinely think?"

Zeke looked from one to another. "Think what?"

Regina returned her gaze to him. "There were rumors probably about thirty years ago that a tiger and tigress had returned. That they were to start a…" Regina faltered, and Ryker looked amused.

"In the wild, believe it or not, a group of tigers is called a streak or an ambush," Ryker drawled. He could believe it, thought Zeke. It sounded ridiculous enough.

"But tiger shifters are always named after the first one. The *Khan*," Regina clarified. "Like a pack or a clan." She looked at Ryker. "The pack is called a khan, but the alpha is also called *the* Khan."

"If it's true, he's in unbelievable danger," Ryker said.

Zeke was trying to keep up with this. "But why? Didn't you just say he was rare?"

Regina sighed. "The power of the Khan is incomparable. For example, I would have no choice but to do exactly as he commands."

Zeke looked incredulously at Regina. No one told her to do anything. She smiled as if reading his thoughts. "And I would be honored to do so."

"And you think Bodhi is a tiger shifter?" It was inconceivable. He remembered the scared, miserable boy. "If he's that badass, why are his uncles getting away with beating on him?"

"Because he doesn't know," Ryker said. "Somehow, and I have no idea how or why, but that young man has no idea he's anything other than a shifter anomaly. Some despised mixed breed. He has no idea. They obviously don't know what he is, they think he's an omega."

"But I thought he *was* an omega?" Zeke said.

Regina glanced at Ryker and even Zeke could see the question in her eyes. "I trust him with Emmett's life," Ryker said simply.

Zeke didn't have the chance to acknowledge the huge degree of trust that had always been unspoken between them when Regina carried on. "The rumor was that the tiger pair eventually had a cub and that he disappeared. If it's true and he is the Khan-re or heir his word, his decree, would be second only to the Khan himself. Although he may not have been imprinted," she added.

Regina saw his confusion, so she carried on. "Imprinted by the pack. It's a ceremony of legend and happens at birth, but it's when he becomes the Khan-re or heir. It teaches him the meaning of the khan, not to *be* the Khan. That comes later, obviously."

"Are you saying that Bhodi somehow is the alpha-heir or tiger equivalent?" Zeke clarified. "And because he wasn't imprinted by his pack he doesn't know?" Regina nodded solemnly.

"I guess not being able to shift wouldn't help either," Zeke said.

"Omega tigers do shift," Ryker said. "But not if he hasn't been imprinted."

"It's the other reason for the imprinting," Regina explained. "The Khan imprints on the cub and brings on his first shift."

Zeke's eyebrows rose. "As a baby?"

Regina nodded. "He won't be able to shift unless he is mated by an alpha. Powerful alphas can also bring on first shifts in any omegas who are able to. Bears for example. Except for the Khan-re," Regina added. "If the stories are correct not even his father—the Khan—can bring on his first shift now. Only his alpha-mate would be able to do that now."

Ryker rubbed his scruff and sighed, pinning Zeke with his gaze. "You can't tell anyone. I'm not even going to share it with my betas until it becomes necessary. This has to remain with us three. We have to get him away from there."

Ryker and Regina both looked at Zeke questioningly. Zeke took a moment, then he nodded. They weren't asking for ideas; they were asking for agreement.

And he was all in.

# Chapter Ten

"You're smiling."

Darriel looked up at Emmett, knowing it was true.

Emmett sat down. "Could the reason possibly be that that hunk of an alpha is being large and in charge and he just sent you a look that should have seared your eyeballs?"

"Eww," Kai commented, tucking into a large plate of cheesy fries. "That's your dad you're talking about."

Emmett sniggered. "I didn't say it seared my eyeballs."

"Can we stop talking about eyeballs?" Darriel asked, going from hot and bothered to feeling a little queasy. The smell of the fries wasn't helping either.

"Gran likes him," Emmett said.

Kai snorted. "And doctor 'darling' likes your gran." He shuddered. "I don't even want to think about that."

Emmett smiled. "I want her to be happy. She's been on her own for a long time."

"Emmett," Darriel reproved. "They just met, and Griffin isn't a shifter." He clicked his fingers. "No instant thing."

"And the whole panther mating rule thing," Kai pointed out.

Emmett shrugged. "She might be a banana."

Kai groaned. "This is one of your jokes, isn't it?" He looked at Darriel. "Can't you do something?"

"Roll with it," Darriel decreed, and looked at Emmett expectantly. Emmett sniggered.

"He finds her *a-pealing*."

Kai threw a fry at Emmett's head.

TJ and Sam came into the kitchen. Sam was quiet and nodding. TJ seemed to be upset. He was ranting about security and the fact that Sam needed to get his act together. That he was here to protect the omegas, not moon over them. They all looked at each other then back at Sam. Sam chose that moment to look over at them and *winked*.

Kai stifled a giggle. Darriel and Emmett stared open-mouthed at each other. The two betas left the kitchen with their coffees.

"Do you think that's about Louis?" Darriel asked.

Emmett sighed. "I actually managed to talk to him yesterday. Dinah takes him his food, so I persuaded her to let me."

"Do you know where he's from?"

Emmett shook his head. "No one knows. It was Sam who found him when he was out hunting. He had to carry him back. Louis is so terrified, Marco can only see him when Dinah's there. He won't tell anyone anything other than his name."

"But he's letting Sam see him?" Darriel asked.

Kai nodded. "You know Sam is like Marco's trainee; well when Marco found out Louis was able to see Sam without going into a near panic attack, he decided to let Sam see to him."

"TJ obviously doesn't like it," Darriel said.

"He's got his own problems," Emmett replied.

Darriel tuned them out and his thoughts returned, as ever, to his human alpha. All the omegas called Zeke that. It was a mixture of teasing and genuine respect. He acted like an alpha, even the other adult shifters treated him like one. "What will you do when Josie is ready for school?"

Emmett and Kai both turned to him, looking puzzled. "What do you mean?" Emmett asked.

"It was something Zeke said. What if Karina wants to learn to play the piano or compete in the Olympics?"

"I'm pretty sure that'd be cheating," Kai said. "Shifter strength?"

Darriel waved a hand. "Bad example. But what if Maddox wants to fly airplanes? Join the air force?" Kai tilted his head consideringly. "Zeke told me that at the moment, the only thing our children are being taught is how to *survive* in a human world. How to keep secrets." He leaned forward and plucked Emmy out of her stroller before she could announce she was awake, and no one seemed to have noticed. "He said he wants to make sure they learn to thrive. To give them the same opportunities human kids get. He's even got their colleges picked out."

It was humbling and he didn't know what he'd done to deserve this sort of attention from Zeke. For a brief moment, he was back trudging in the forest clutching his mom's hand. She was telling him how special he was. How omegas provided the cohesion for everyone. He'd paused and looked at her in complete confusion. "Con...huh?"

"*Cohesion*," his mom repeated. "Omegas are the glue that holds a pack together. You're a very lucky boy."

But he hadn't felt lucky.

Not the first time he was drugged.

Not the first time he was beaten.

Not the first time he was raped.

And especially not the times he had lost the babies.

"He's right." Kai said, looking at Emmett, and for one awful moment Darriel thought he'd said that out loud, but then he realized they were talking about colleges, not *rape*.

"Dad actually mentioned something like this a few weeks ago, after Josie was born. Said he was going to get her a Braves shirt because she would be a star player for them. I didn't think about it at the time because..." Emmett shrugged.

"But he's got a point," Kai said quietly. "I don't want Maddox to go through what I did. I want him to be able to do whatever he wants."

Emmett held out his hand and curled his little finger. "Pinky swear. Omega Club secret promise. We make it happen." They both did the same.

"He also said we need to prepare for when the world finds out about us."

"I don't know how they don't now," Kai said and chewed his lip.

"Because that's what the shifter council does," Emmett said thoughtfully. "It's their only focus."

"You all look really serious," Chrissy commented, walking toward them.

Emmett tapped the side of his nose. "Secret omega stuff."

She nodded seriously, then winked. "Understood, boss." Ryker, Zeke and Regina walked into the kitchen, Regina making a bee-line for Emmett and Josie.

"I think omegas are going to save the world," Kai said cryptically, stood and gathered Maddox. "But we're going for a nap until we're asked to do so." He grinned and left.

Darriel noticed the moment Zeke turned from talking to Ryker and spotted him. Zeke's eyes darkened and a wave of pure lust rolled over Darriel. It felt almost like a heat, but Zeke was human and couldn't cause that. His body seemed to clench from the inside out. Zeke tilted his head as he looked at Darriel and a slow smile curved his lips. Ryker—who had still been talking to Zeke—suddenly noticed Zeke was no longer listening, rolled his eyes, and followed Regina to Emmett and Josie. Darriel watched as Zeke stalked in his direction. His laser-focused dark eyes almost predator-like. Another tremor made goose bumps bloom on Darriel's skin. Zeke plucked Emmy from Darriel's arms and nodded to the stroller. He dropped a kiss on Emmy's forehead as she stared at him with huge brown eyes. "Come on, gorgeous. Let's see what you think of my room. Lots of books."

Darriel wanted to ask questions. Like, how did the meeting go? What was the plan? Did they think they could rescue Bodhi? But the look on Zeke's face silenced him. He shivered, every nerve ending felt alive. Zeke frowned.

"You're cold?"

Darriel shook his head and felt his cheeks warm. Whatever it was, it was giving him all sorts of incredible thoughts...*needs...wants*. Zeke smiled a little and they walked to his room. Zeke opened the door so Darriel could push the stroller in. Karina was asleep but he knew Emmy wasn't. He turned to see if Zeke wanted him to take her and gaped a little in surprise. Zeke was standing, balancing Emmy against him securely with her head laid against his chest. He was rubbing small circles on her diapered bottom with his other hand, and she had her eyes closed. His eyes smarted a little to see the big man holding Emmy so securely, but then the rest of his body reminded him it was a huge turn on. Big strong men and babies? It was a no brainer. Zeke gently settled Emmy in the stroller and covered her with the blanket, then straightened and stepped up to Darriel. He cupped Darriel's cheek in one of his large hands, the other arm snaking around Darriel's waist.

"I love it when I see that reaction."

"What one?" Darriel licked his lips; Zeke's mouth was so close, his body so warm and pressing against him in so many interesting places. His whole body seemed to thrum.

"To see you blush, or not exactly. Your skin is so pretty, but when you react to a compliment or a feeling it gets darker here." He smoothed a thumb over Darriel's cheekbones. "It's not very obvious but when I notice, I always want to know what caused it." Darriel met Zeke's gaze, his blue-gray eyes darkening almost to slate. "Or what makes your eyes sparkle." Zeke murmured and lowered his head.

Their lips met so gently, almost a question in the soft touch of Zeke's mouth. Darriel moaned and Zeke pressed harder, a small nip on his bottom lip to open, and a soothing lick of Zeke's tongue in acknowledgement when he did so.

"I wanted to kiss you for such a long time," Zeke murmured as he peppered kisses along Darriel's throat. Darriel's heart seemed to skip and then go into overdrive.

"You did?"

"Uh-huh." Darriel closed his eyes as Zeke's sure fingers started to undress him slowly. By the time Zeke undid his zip to pull down his jeans, Darriel was so hard he gasped in relief when his cock bounced free. Zeke closed his hand around it instantly, using the tip of his finger to catch the precum and ease the glide through his hand.

"I love how responsive you are. How you let me do this, touch you."

"I love your touch. You were the first person ever to really notice me."

Zeke faltered, immediately letting go. He looked like he was debating what to say and Darriel got it. "I didn't mean I'm letting you do this out of some weird sense of gratitude. I'm safe here. The girls are safe. This has nothing to do with that." *This was so much more.* "I meant the way you look at me. My body notices. All of my body." He finished stripping them both, brought Zeke's hand back to his engorged cock and moaned at the touch of his fingers. He led Zeke to the bed and sank down, pulling Zeke with him until they stretched out next to each other.

He trailed a finger down Zeke's bare chest and scraped his nipple. Zeke shuddered and his cock jerked against Darriel's thigh. He *liked* that and bent his head, closing his lips around Zeke's nipple and sucking. Zeke moaned and Darriel, thrilled he could get such a response, reached down and took Zeke's now leaking cock in his fingers. He loved the velvety feel of skin over rock-hard muscle. That was Zeke all over, and he whimpered in anticipation as Zeke suddenly reared up and flipped Darriel on his back. Zeke's hand traced a line from Darriel's throat all the way to his balls and he bit his lip to avoid begging. Fuck, could this be any more perfect?

Zeke took charge and Darriel reveled in it. He pinned Darriel's arms above his head. It was nothing to do with size or even physical control, because while Zeke was a strong man, he wasn't a shifter.

Darriel's wolf might be dormant but he could still put Zeke on his back. Groaning, he arched in invitation as all sorts of glorious images filtered through his mind, and he reached for Zeke's lips and urgent kisses.

Zeke returned them just as hungrily, desperately, until Darriel gloried in submitting because he wanted to, not because he *had* to. Not because the alternative meant pain. He wanted Zeke to direct his body in pleasure. Take what he needed. Darriel hissed at the initial penetration, even though his omega slick smoothed the glide. He hissed because it was so damn good. Because it made him feel owned. Because it made him feel *mated*. Darriel was so hard. He felt Zeke falter in his desire, but still reach out to touch him. Even when his mind was exploding with utter lust, Zeke still wanted Darriel's pleasure. It was that thought that pushed him over the edge, even before Zeke's hand fisted his swollen cock. Fireworks exploded in his body. White light blinded him even behind closed eyelids. And then it was just so damn good he wanted to laugh and cry at the same time.

Except it wasn't him crying.

Darriel didn't register the first sound, maybe not even the second, but the third muffled sob tore through him. His beautiful strong man was crying and, even more heartbreaking, trying to stifle the noise. "Zeke, sweetheart," Darriel whispered as Zeke slid out of him and rolled away. Darriel followed, gathering him up unprotestingly in his arms.

"You can't." Zeke tried to turn away, struggling half-heartedly, more concerned with muffling the noise than accepting comfort.

"Shh," Darriel soothed, holding him even tighter until Zeke sagged into his arms, tears falling quietly, but unrelenting. He felt Zeke falter, gulp a breath. "What is it?" A cold, hard ball settled in the pit of his stomach. "If you've changed your mind about us—" But he couldn't finish the words. He could have bawled himself. He felt Zeke shake his head against his shoulder and breathed a sigh of relief.

"I—" Zeke swallowed. "I—forced you," he choked out. "I held you down." Thoughts whirled in Darriel's brain. "The same..."

"The same as what?" Darriel whispered. Somehow, he didn't think that this was about him.

"I wasn't strong enough. There was this guy"—Zeke gasped for air as if it was finite—"that held both my wrists in one hand and hit me with the other as if it was *nothing* to him. I was helpless. I couldn't move. He held me up against a wall with just one hand until I couldn't breathe and there was nothing I could do. They wanted me to beg. To apologize. To admit I was helpless. They hit me until I *pissed myself*." The last horrified words came out on an agonized wail and Darriel finally understood. He wrapped his arms around Zeke while he shook, thanking the heavens the girls didn't wake up. It had been this. Shaming, stripping him of all control. Dehumanizing him, that had hurt Zeke the most, and he was worried the control he had exerted over Darriel was no better.

"Zeke," Darriel whispered after a few more minutes. Zeke didn't respond, so Darriel tried again. "My darling." The huff from Zeke told him he doubted he was Darriel's anything. "Listen to me."

Zeke finally looked at him and Darriel cupped his face, the same gesture that Zeke had done to him so many times. "Shifters will always be physically stronger than humans, but that's nothing to do with why I adored what we just did. I love it when you show me how much you care for me." Zeke blew out a sharp, disbelieving breath. "Apart from it being insanely hot, what you're really asking when you restrain me is to trust you. Trust you to take care of me. Trust you to make every touch special. Trust you to drive me wild with every kiss." Darriel kissed Zeke gently. "And I do. When you dominate me it's every fantasy I ever dared dream come to life."

Zeke didn't reply but Darriel could tell he still wasn't sure. "Do you know what happened to me from the age of fourteen?"

Pain flared in Zeke's eyes, and he lifted up on one elbow, gathering Darriel close. It was instinctive, Zeke didn't even realize what he was doing.

"I've been forced. I've been *raped*. I know what that is, and I certainly know the difference between that and what we just did.

96

What was done to you was monstrous, but I know there wasn't anything else compelling you to do the things you did with me other than knowing deep down it was what I needed. What I *enjoyed*. What we both desired."

Zeke was silent for a minute. "I don't deserve you."

"Really? I think it's the other way around. You're this wildly successful guy. Have a ton of people, businesses, *shifters* relying on you every day to keep delivering, to keep rescuing them, to give them a future. And somehow, you found the time to come and read me stories. *Day after day*, Zeke. Days when I could have happily closed my eyes and *never woken up*." He was angry and brushed the wetness from his eyes. "And you only stopped when I was strong enough to push you away."

"But you did," Zeke said hoarsely. "That shows—"

"That I finally realized I wasn't good enough for you."

Zeke shook his head and pressed a gentle kiss on his lips in just the way he loved. "No, sweetheart. *Never*. You are a delight. A selfless soul that only sees the good in everyone and I'm..." He let go and rolled on his back, staring up at the ceiling. "I'm not good enough to be anywhere near you." He closed his eyes and Darriel stayed silent. This wasn't some self-worth issue like his. This was something different. And as Darriel watched the self-disgust flicker across Zeke's face, he knew he was back with the clan.

"Tell me," he entreated.

Zeke opened desolate eyes and turned his head to face him. "I said *yes*." His voice shook. "I agreed that the clans were monstrous. That Regina was just as bad. That Trina shouldn't be with the Panthera that had murdered Josephine, but that she should be back home with her family. The same family that had known for years where Marco was and had never so much as raised a finger in anger against him." He tried to swallow and rasped. "I promised. I promised that when they found out where she was, I would help them get her back. Or Emmett and Josie might die. I promised because they told me that next time they wouldn't take me, they would take the ones I love." Zeke brought their foreheads together. "And now that includes you. I cannot ever let what happened to me happen to another soul, never mind the ones I would die to keep safe."

Darriel gathered him in his arms while silent tears tracked down both their cheeks. He didn't know what to say, even less what to do. "I think you need to tell Ryker."

"I did, and I don't think he believed me. Or, I tried to warn him," Zeke admitted. "But you're right. I need to spell it out." He looked over to the stroller and smiled as blankets were shuffled about as the occupants stirred. "I can't believe they slept through all that."

Darriel sat up, ready to see to them both. "Are you going to talk to Regina?"

Zeke nodded. "I'm going to do it now." He shot him a look of such love Darriel could have easily cried again, but then he smiled. He didn't know what to do but he was determined to help. Determined to keep them together. Because he'd always doubted he was enough for Zeke. Now he knew he was exactly what his alpha needed.

And he intended to keep it that way.

# Chapter Eleven

Darriel watched Zeke leave. He honestly didn't know what to do, and he was so distracted, he got the girls ready almost on auto-pilot, which he felt guilty for. Hungry, he pushed the stroller toward the kitchen.

Relieved to see Emmett, Kai, and Charles, he went to join them. Emmett smirked. Darriel allowed it. Both girls were immediately taken off his hands, and he tucked into some of Dinah's lasagna, which he'd never been partial to before, but could have happily eaten another plateful.

"Do you know what the sudden second meeting's about?" Kai asked furtively. Darriel kept his head down because he had a feeling he knew.

"The problem is getting Bodhi or any of the other omegas on their own," Emmett said.

Darriel jerked his head upright. "What other omegas?"

Charles leaned forward. "You don't know? Where have you been for the last couple of hours?" He flushed pink at Darriel's sheepish grin and waved a hand. "Never mind."

"So, major update," Emmett said lowering his voice. "Red's on his way back after scoping the place. Apparently Bodhi isn't the only omega the Davies brothers have. They've bought a whole pack house of them."

"You're kidding me," Darriel said, aghast.

"I wish I was," Emmett answered. "The only reason they parade Bodhi about is because technically he's legal. Red found the compound the brothers have. He reckons at least twenty different omegas from different shifter groups."

"But why?" Darriel blurted out. "What are they hoping to prove?"

Emmett huffed. "You know non-shifters don't have the gene or whatever that can get us pregnant?"

Kai and Darriel both agreed. Charles was listening silently as usual. "Well, from what I understand, Porter is convinced he has it. He's trying to get them all pregnant, and Paxton is just taking care of the leftovers."

"Why though? Why does Porter want a bunch of pregnant omegas?"

"His own army. He's like some conspiracy nut job. Convinced the shifter world is planning a takeover. To treat humans as slaves. Ryker thinks that's why they want the land so close to ours."

"How did they get the omegas though?" Darriel asked.

Emmett scowled. "Same as ever, they bought them."

"This was one of the places Riggs sold the omegas to?" Darriel said quietly. Dead, and he was still fucking them over.

*You're good for nothing else.* He could still hear Riggs's grunt as he rammed into him.

Emmett nodded quietly but his eyes were full of pain.

"Which will be guarded like Fort Knox," Kai added morosely.

"And Ryker told me that Bodhi is terrified of him."

"He was," Darriel said reluctantly. "It was like he smelled shifter and panicked. And he'd rather stay with the brothers even though they hurt him." In a way, Darriel understood. The alphas always had the power. Humans, especially bullies, could physically make someone do something with a gun, but they weren't as frightening as some alphas. Darriel knew that. "So what are we going to do about it?"

Three pairs of eyes focused on him. "What could we do?" Charles asked carefully.

"Well, they can't do anything," Kai said. "No alphas the size of ours could walk into an omega compound. Even Chrissy looks threatening. They wouldn't get anywhere near it. And then, what if all the omegas feel the same as Bodhi does? What if they refuse to leave?"

"Unless they have the backing of the shifter council," Emmett agreed. "And even then, people might get hurt."

"But what if I could talk to them?" Darriel said. "I saw the guns they had. We just had a shootout where we lost omegas. I don't want that to happen again."

"I could try," Charles said. "It's only fair. I don't—" He shut up, but they all knew what word he'd cut off. That he didn't have kids, so he didn't *count*.

"Actually, it will have to be me," Darriel said, and all three outraged pairs of eyes stared at him. "I know Bodhi. He recognized me." Emmett opened his mouth then closed it again.

"But—"

"I have the girls?" Darriel asked, correctly guessing what he was going to say. He smiled. "What if Karina does want to be a concert pianist?" And he saw understanding in every gaze. "I don't want them to just survive. It's the same thing over and over again."

Emmett leaned forward. "And what if you get in? Then what? It seems like a bad plan."

Darriel chuckled. "It's a crazy plan." He leaned forward. "Come on Omega Club, what are we going to do?"

"I have an idea," Kai said, "but we're going to be dead when our alphas find out."

They fell silent as Fox sauntered into the kitchen, mock-saluted them all, grabbed a pot of coffee that Dinah handed him, and left.

Darriel glanced at Charles just to see his reaction and was briefly taken aback by the longing on Charles's face before he saw Darriel looking and masked it quickly. Darriel didn't think, despite how Fox had seemed at first, that there was any attraction between them, but that clearly wasn't the case, at least with Charles. Darriel reached over and squeezed his hand.

"Are you okay?"

"I would be if I was fifteen years younger and able to have babies."

Emmett leaned forward. "He actually said that?"

"No," Charles smiled. "He doesn't have to. Anyway, the first problem is how to get to the camp."

If anyone was taken aback by the quick change of subject, they didn't show it. "No," said Darriel. "The first problem is how to get out of here."

"Because none of us can shift," Emmett said gloomily.

Kai snorted. "You wouldn't get past the claw patrolling the grounds anyway." Since Regina had found out Emmett was her grandson, she had claw members here permanently to protect the grounds. It worked because Ryker had more wolves to pull from for the rescues if they needed it.

Emmett looked over at Dinah, who was walking in and out of the cooler writing things down. "It's Wednesday."

Kai looked blankly at him.

"She'd never go for it," Darriel hissed. There was no way.

"Go for what?" Kai asked impatiently.

"Every Wednesday Dinah goes into Asheville to the Farmer's market. It's why she's making a list." Emmett whispered.

"And checking it twice," Kai singsonged, then saw everyone's exasperated reaction and shrugged.

"There's no way she'd take me," Darriel whispered. "And we can't go when the brothers are going to be there."

"No," Emmett agreed, "but we can as soon as they meet our alphas again. It's Christmas next month and I have to buy presents. She knows I'm used to existing in a human world. We're not in danger of shifting, and we can say it's a surprise so she's not to say anything, and you need some things for the girls."

"She's going to kill us when she finds out we've lied," Darriel added gloomily. *But there's nothing else I can do.*

"Emmett," Kai sighed. "You know full well there's no way Dinah would ever take the alpha-mate on a shopping trip when we're being attacked on all sides. She'd never do it without Ryker's permission, and he'd insist on an armed guard. Emmett slumped and looked ruefully at Darriel. They all knew he was right.

"You said you had an idea." Darriel pointed out.

"It's a bad one."

"What is it?" Darriel pressed.

"Trina's coming next week for Thanksgiving. She'd smuggle one of us out."

"Too far away," Darriel said. "And she's protected more than we are."

Emmett nodded, held out his little finger and they hooked them. He glanced at Charles and Kai. "You're on baby duty." Then he wandered over to Dinah.

"So, I get there when we find out when the meeting's happening. Somehow get in without being noticed," Darriel said shaking his head. "Then what?"

"They're not shifters so they won't be able to scent you," Charles pointed out. "And If you go when the guys are meeting the brothers there's no one to recognize you either."

"But how do I get in?"

"You could name drop," Charles said carefully.

Darriel frowned.

"He's right," Kai said almost apologetically. "You know as much about Riggs as the rest. Say you've been thrown out. Say Riggs was good to you. Who's going to call you on it?"

"Okay," Darriel nodded and watched Emmett talking to Dinah, and her vehemently shaking her head. "That's not going to happen."

Kai and Charles looked at each other. "This is an incredibly bad idea. It has more holes than smelly cheese."

Charles huffed. "Bodhi might not even be there."

But there must be something they could do. He knew Bodhi would listen to him if he got the chance to talk. He just had absolutely no idea how to make that happen.


Zeke clicked his phone off and stood just outside Ryker's office. He'd promised Darriel he'd talk to Ryker but May had called him with as much news as she had been able to find out about the brothers, and to tell him he had missed three business meetings. May was good but at some point, he had to go back to work. His phone rang again, and he answered it quickly, assuming it was May with another update.

"Coleman." There was total silence and Zeke looked at the screen. Withheld number. "Who is this?" He would hang up.

Then the voice from his nightmares slid into his ear. "Well, well, Mr. Coleman. It's been some time since I heard your voice."

Zeke curled his fingers tighter around his phone to stop them from shaking. "What do you want?"

The smooth laugh made him want to throw up. "I've missed our time together. I think we should meet. I want reassurances that you still feel the same."

"Reassurances?" His heart took up a beat so loud it echoed in his ear.

"Yes, you remember your promises and how easy it was to take you? That next time we wouldn't bother with you but with your son? Maybe Josephine's namesake? Or maybe we should come up there? Find out what seems to be keeping you away from your many businesses? We don't like you being there all this time. It makes us want to find out what the attraction is."

This time Zeke couldn't even respond. Then he heard metal clanking. The distinct rattle as chains were slid through something. Sweat broke out on his skin and his vision grayed. The pain. They'd strung him up, then the man had always tightened his chains just before the beating started again. There was a name for it. The noise that reminded him of the pain and caused a psychological reaction. He knew it, he just couldn't seem to think of it right at that moment.

"We understand our mutual friend will be visiting the compound this week."

Zeke thought he'd misheard for a moment. "Visiting?" he rasped and clutched at the wall in front of him. What the hell? Trina was coming here?

"There's no way she would be here without her protection." There was a laugh down the phone.

"Leave the claw to us." There was a pause. "However, our immediate needs have changed and there may be an easier way. You have met Paxton and Porter Davies regarding their claim on your land."

Zeke stared at the phone. What the *fuck*? "Why do you care?"

"We have no interest in them whatsoever. However, we want the omega, Bodhi."

Zeke felt like every drop of blood in his body pooled at his feet. "Since when do panthers want omegas?"

"None of your concern. You wait until you are called by them. You won't need to inform us because we will know. You go to the compound, collect the omega, meet us, and we will take him from you. Assuming those conditions are met, we will never bother you or your family again. If, however, you cross us or think to become inventive, we will make sure you have a front-row seat to your son's torture and execution." The phone clicked off.

Zeke tried to swallow. *How?*

"Zeke?" Zeke lifted his head as the door opened, hearing Ryker swear, and felt an arm go around him. "You look like shit. I think you've been overdoing it and need to sit this one out."

Zeke straightened and pulled away from Ryker. He couldn't even cope with that sort of touch at the moment. "I'm fine. What one?"

Ryker looked incredulous. "You're a stubborn bastard."

Zeke nodded in agreement and pulled himself up straighter. "What's happened?"

"Red's on his way back. His news isn't good. He told me briefly, but I think we should wait to hear it from him."

Zeke made sure his expression didn't change. He knew he had to say something, but the words stuck in his throat. He fisted his hands by his sides to stop them shaking, took a deep breath then walked into Ryker's office. Chrissy was talking to Regina and they both glanced up as he entered, but then went back to a map Chrissy was holding. He had to speak. He had to say something now. "Regina—" The door opened again and when he turned, he saw Red enter the room. Red was breathing hard and just buttoning his shirt.

"It's confirmed they've got more than him."

Ryker's head snapped up. "How many?"

"I could smell at least eighteen scent signatures, all shifters. The guards I saw are human."

"You followed them," Regina acknowledged.

Zeke watched Ryker glance at Regina and the small nod she gave him. Then Ryker casually got Red a coffee and explained to Red and Chrissy who they thought Bodhi was.

Red was silent for quite a few minutes after. Chrissy didn't seem to have a reply either. "How likely is this?" Red asked eventually.

"Can you tell what sort of shifter he is?" Ryker asked, as if in answer.

Red shook his head. "But I wasn't as close as you."

"You're still an alpha," Ryker pointed out. "I'm betting you could name the type of shifters in the compound you just visited and I'm also hoping you were farther away."

Red sighed. "Fourteen wolves. Three bears. One I wasn't sure of."

Ryker didn't need to say Red had just proved his point. Zeke met Ryker's eyes. Chrissy sighed. "Do you think this is to do with Riggs? There were omegas we never found, both from the cave where we found Michael's body last year and when Mills River was taken over." Riggs, the bastard responsible for not only murdering Ryker's human mother, but also for Darriel's injuries and the omega trafficking that they had hoped they had put a stop to with his death, even if they had never found all the omegas.

"It looks like it," Regina snapped out. Zeke glanced over and saw the fury in her gaze. Suspicion coiled in his gut. Why did their experience with Riggs anger Regina?

He shrugged. "I doubt Riggs was ever a threat to the clan."

Ryker sent him an incredulous look and Regina seemed to still. Then she looked up and speared him with her gaze. "I will forgive you that because of your recent treatment by a clan, but if you ever intimate again by one thought or deed that I wouldn't do everything in my power not only to help my grandson but also the only thing I have left to remind me of Josie, I will take you outside and kill you myself."

Zeke wasn't proud of the step he took backwards in reaction to her anger, but then, he wasn't proud of his assumption either. He was so rattled he'd completely forgotten Regina had in fact saved Emmett's life.

He might disagree with the clans, but she had proved over and over she was on their side and willing to put herself in jeopardy to show it. Shame licked at his skin like a burn. Wasn't he just proving by his reaction that Josie had been right to leave him? That she couldn't trust him?

This had to stop. He should be better than this, and he needed, *had* to tell them. He couldn't protect them on his own. He stepped forward into Regina's space, but she didn't back down. He reached out and took her hand. A wary disbelief shadowed her eyes, but she didn't pull away.

"I need to tell you something, two somethings. I was about to when Red arrived, but it's long overdue." He raised his eyes to Ryker, including him in the apology. "I told Ryker, but I was so ashamed I hoped you would never know." He felt the gentle tightening of Regina's fingers and, reminding him of Josie, it gave him strength. "I broke.

What they did—" He closed his mouth, petrified that a sob would come out, and struggled to control himself. "I agreed to anything just to have them let me go, and it wasn't just the pain, although that was indescribable. It was the humiliation. That I was nothing. That this shifter had the strength to incapacitate me when he barely looked like he was breaking a sweat. And he probably wasn't."

Regina's eyes turned from anger to empathy.

He took a steadying breath. "I agreed to help them get Trina back." Regina let go and Zeke didn't blame her. He wouldn't want to touch him either. The disbelieving snort from Ryker had him turning around. "I tried to tell you," he protested. He was ready to take the deserved disgust from his best friend. Ryker shook his head.

"Damn it all, Zeke." He took a step closer. "You had to say whatever you could to get free, but I've known you twenty years buddy. You have more integrity in your little finger than most people do in their entire bodies." He put a hand on Zeke's shoulder. "You have my back and I have yours. Always have, always will."

"There's something else." He felt physically ill and sat down before his legs gave way. "The man, panther, whatever. It was always the same one. I never saw any other faces. I thought he didn't care that I could identify him because he was going to kill me anyway."

"I have people investigating," Regina said. "I'm just having to do it quietly because there's no proof."

*"He just called me."*

Everyone fell silent. Regina leaned forward. "What did he want?"

"He started taunting me about Trina at first. He knew she's coming here next week for Thanksgiving."

"Emmett invited Trina for Thanksgiving," Regina confirmed. "I may change my own plans."

"I didn't know that," Ryker admitted "but the claw will be with her."

"He said I didn't need to worry about them."

Regina hissed in a breath.

"He hinted at other things. Why I'm still here. What's keeping me here. And that they don't like it." He stared at her for a moment, unable to mention Darriel's name, and watched her absorb everything, then meet his gaze. "Then he said they had changed their minds and had other needs."

Regina froze.

"He said I have to meet the Davies brothers on my own. Go to the compound. Get Bodhi and then hand him over. They said if I do that, our business would be concluded and they would never threaten my family again."

He glanced up in shame at Ryker. "I've heard the omegas tease me, calling me the human alpha, but at the first test I let you down, betrayed—"

"No, you fucking well didn't," Ryker snapped out. "No one, no shifter, no one knows what they'd do in the same situation."

"Marco—"

"Was held for hours, not for *ten days*. He was beaten but then they changed their mind. If you had been subjected to the same, you would have reacted in the same manner." Ryker hunched down next to Zeke. "You've got it wrong. Shifters aren't superhuman. No one knows what they would do to protect their mate and family unless they're pushed to it. Emmett means everything to me. I couldn't choose. No one can, and that doesn't matter whether they're a shifter or not."

"And now you have someone else to protect," Regina pointed out in a voice so gentle he was shocked. He also knew he had to say something else and met her gaze.

"I'm sorry. I've been blaming you for something that wasn't your fault for a long time. I think I was looking for anyone to blame but myself. I always felt if Josie had trusted me, she could have told me. It's like I was always less. Just a human. They proved that." He'd been trying to measure up against shifters all his life and *failed* every time.

"I think she would have told you. I think finding out she was pregnant made her panic. I don't think it was a lack of trust. I never doubted she loved you, she was just scared what the clan would do to you if they found out. We all know Barry put that fear into her for his own selfish reasons."

Zeke returned her sorrowful gaze. He wasn't the only one who had lost Josie. "We need to take him out. We need to get the omegas, but I can't live with this threat over my mate and family. I will do whatever I have to, to make sure they're safe. Then there's Trina."

"And whoever told them," Regina clipped out. She'd gone from distraught and betrayed to furious in a heartbeat. Good. They needed a furious Regina.

"And Bodhi," Chrissy added.

Red swore. "The compound is locked up tight. They won't smell wolf shifters, but any stranger would be a threat. Especially anyone your size." He nodded to Ryker.

"Or yours," Ryker said ruefully which was true.

"And your claw would be even worse," Zeke said regretfully. "I don't care what they say. I won't risk anyone else, and it stops now. As soon as the brothers call, I'm going to meet them on my own."

And he had to leave. He couldn't risk the claw coming to see why he was here and finding out about Darriel. It would kill him, but Zeke was clearly toxic. He needed to stay away.

And he couldn't tell him *why*.

# Chapter Twelve

"I have to go."

Darriel stared at Zeke. They'd just had supper. Zeke had been quiet, but Darriel knew what an awful day he'd had so he hadn't pushed. "Go where?"

Zeke stood up and kissed Karina's head and laid her in the crib. Emmy, for once, had fallen asleep before her sister. He smiled gently and tugged Darriel toward him. "I have to go to work. I've been away for over two weeks and while May is great, it's not fair. I have investors coming early tomorrow and I need to prepare for it."

"You're going tonight?" Darriel pressed against him as if he could somehow make him stay. "Will you be back tomorrow night?"

Darriel heard the pause and didn't need the subsequent "I can't" to understand. He lifted his head and met Zeke's eyes, and every doubt about how Zeke felt rushed back with a vengeance.

"I'll be as quick as I can, then we need to talk properly without all this going on." Darriel nodded but he didn't think he could speak. Zeke made a pained sound in the back of his throat and clutched Darriel tight. He wrapped his arms around him and Darriel fought back the sob. "I don't have a choice, but when I get back, we're going to talk about having our own house built up here."

Darriel gasped. "We are?" He snuggled into Zeke's warm chest, feeling his heartbeat return to normal.

"When I said we have to talk it wasn't some euphemism for saying goodbye. It was about planning the rest of our lives." Zeke leaned back so he could see Darriel's face. "You have my heart, so you need to keep it safe for when I get back."

Darriel could barely speak. "You promise?"

Zeke smiled and kissed him. A lazy exploration of warm lips that sent all sorts of delicious ideas down Darriel's body. Zeke chuckled as if he'd heard him. "Make sure you keep those babies safe." His expression grew serious. "And eat. This body belongs to me, and I expect you to look after it." It was such an outrageously Zeke thing to say that Darriel smiled, despite everything. Zeke stepped away. "Stay here and warm. Ryker will see me out. I'll text you tomorrow."

"Text me when you get there," Darriel practically demanded.

"Of course." Then he turned and left. Darriel sank down onto the bed and hugged himself tightly, for once wishing Emmy wasn't asleep and could distract him. Zeke had been a sweetheart, but he had an awful feeling there was something else he wasn't saying. Something Darriel wouldn't like. Something he would *fear*.


Four days later, Zeke was still gone.

Zeke had insisted he had to go back and see to pressing business matters, but Darriel had been suspicious and now four days on, was even more so. He knew something else was going on, but not even Emmett had been able to get anything out of Ryker. The truly terrifying thought was that Zeke was trying to make himself accessible either to the Davies brothers or the clan. Who was going to protect him though?

He yawned and rolled over in bed just as he felt his phone vibrate. He glanced at it. Five a.m.? The girls were asleep, and he supposed he should be, but his bed seemed very empty. He wanted to move into Zeke's room, but he couldn't because Zeke hadn't asked him.

*"Are you awake?"*

Darriel smiled at the text. *"Yes, but the girls aren't."*

*"Sorry, did I wake u?"*

*"No. I was just missing u. When r u coming home?"* There. He'd said *home*.

*"Soon."* Darriel sighed. Not today?

*"Miss u."*

*"Miss u 2. Give girls a kiss from me."*

"Love you." But Darriel whispered the words. He didn't want to put pressure—or any more pressure—on Zeke. Not until this was all done. It was like a huge cloud hanging over their heads.

They were planning a huge Thanksgiving feast for everyone. Trina and Regina were coming later that day, and so was Dr. "Darling" as they secretly called Dr. G. Emmett was convinced he was some sort of one-man dating agency and that his gran and the doctor needed to get together. Maybe Darriel had time to go grab a shower before the girls woke up? He slid quietly out of bed and went to the bathroom, stripping off the ratty T-shirt and shorts he normally slept in, and stood in front of the mirror giving himself a critical once over. Then he did a double take. What the hell? He prodded his chest. His pecs were puffy and his nipples large, or larger. He tried to remember if he'd banged into anything that would cause a bruise or swelling but came up blank.

He had to take the girls to see Marco tomorrow for their check up and he wasn't looking forward to it. He knew the girls were thriving, but he'd started getting pointed looks from Emmett and Kai. He wasn't eating, or not enough. He just felt weird. All wrong in his skin and he didn't know what it was. And now there seemed to be something else. He looked down at his chest. Should he mention it? How embarrassing would that be? But what if there was something wrong? It was noticeable and he knew for sure Zeke would spot it. Heat seemed to rush through Darriel's body at that thought and his cock, already hard when he'd woken up, gave another twitch. Zeke hadn't said he couldn't touch himself, and Darriel had almost been disappointed he hadn't, but it wasn't his own hand he wanted. He stepped in the shower and ran a hand over his nipples, gasping at the sudden tingling. He wasn't especially responsive there, well not unless Zeke touched them, but they seemed incredibly sensitive. Zeke seemed to make his whole body an entire mass of trembling need. All he needed to do was spear him with those blue-gray eyes and he was a goner. He let his hand drop and quickly washed, gritting his teeth and fighting the urge not to play with himself. He told himself he was a dumbass for not taking advantage of some quiet time but stepped out and wrapped a huge towel around his middle.

His phone vibrated again, and he reached over to the counter for it. Thrilled, Darriel answered the call. "I was in the shower."

A second's silence then a groan came down the line. "Not fair. Now I'm going to be thinking of that all day."

Darriel smiled and, feeling a little daring, stroked a hand over his nipple, unable to contain the gasp.

"What are you doing?" The question was insistent, an order almost.

"I touched my nipple," Darriel admitted. "They're sensitive this morning and I was thinking of you."

"Really?" Zeke asked. "What are you imagining?" Darriel shivered at Zeke's deep voice.

"That it's your hands touching me."

"Are you still in the bathroom?"

Darriel nodded but then realized Zeke couldn't see him and whispered. "Yes."

"Naked?" Zeke's voice seemed to glide over his skin like silk.

"Mmm, towel."

"Drop it." Darriel unfastened it and let it fall. His heart started beating a little faster and he stared at himself in the mirror, imagining it was Zeke looking at him.

"Are you hard, baby? Thinking of me, thinking of my lips licking at your skin?"

Darriel whimpered, his hand trailing down his abdomen.

"Take your cock, imagine my fingers curling around you, squeezing, stroking."

"Zeke," Darriel gasped out in a strangled voice and closed his eyes pretending they were Zeke's fingers. How he would stroke his thumb over the tip of Darriel's cock then push it between Darriel's lips so he could taste himself. He put the phone down and pressed the speaker. Zeke's warm, seductive voice seemed to fill the room.

"That's right, baby. Feel the ache in your balls. Feel the scrape of my nails as I tug them. Feel my finger heading toward your hole. How slick you are. How empty. How you need me to fill you right up."

"P-please," Darriel begged, not even sure how he was still standing.

"I've got you," Zeke murmured. "Take your finger and imagine it's mine." Darriel let his head fall forward, leaning against the wall. He couldn't quite reach and let out a low whine of protest. He heard Zeke chuckle. "Spread the towel on the floor and lie down. Put the phone near you and close your eyes." Darriel did exactly as he was instructed. "Now bend your knees and reach under you."

Darriel gasped. "So-so good."

"That's right baby. Now with your other hand touch your nipples, my lips are on you and I'm teasing them with my teeth. Press hard with your fingers." Darriel did and his cock jerked in response. "That's it. Feel my bite."

He shook. In his mind he was picturing another bite, one on his neck. "Zeke," he pleaded. He wanted that so much.

"Now take your cock. Make sure your hand is nice and slick and hold on because I know how you like a smooth glide. Up and down, that's it. Squeeze the tip. Tug your nipples. Both hands. One on your cock and the other touching your chest. Can you feel the pleasure building?"

Darriel nodded, past being capable of anything but breathless moans and gasps.

"That's it, steady rhythm. Up and down. Feel your belly tightening? Those aching balls lifting? Your heartbeat pounding in your ears, and the pulse in your cock. Nearly there, baby, one more. One more pull and I'm pushing my hard cock inside you."

Darriel's brain seemed to short circuit at the image. He could almost feel Zeke's hands, his mouth, the pressure and the bliss that followed. He arched his back, his hips thrusting and his cock jerking in his grasp. Hot bursts of come hit his belly and coated his fingers and he cried out Zeke's name, lost in desperate pleasure.

"That's it, baby. That's it," Zeke murmured. He was silent for a few seconds as if he knew Darriel needed a moment. "How do you feel?"

Darriel opened his eyes and stared at the bathroom ceiling, feeling his heart rate slow. "I want you home." He needed him. He loved him and the words were so desperate to come out, he didn't know how much longer he could keep them trapped.

"I know." Zeke clicked off. Darriel got up, listened to make sure all was quiet and turned the shower back on. If Zeke didn't come home tomorrow, Darriel would go and get him.


But when the next morning came, Darriel felt dreadful. He knew his eating had been erratic, but he felt sick and shaky, and it was an effort to get the girls ready and push them to the clinic.

"The girls are both doing amazingly well," Marco said and lifted Karina off the scales. "Another ounce and she's going to be a whole eight pounds." He glanced over at Darriel and Darriel smiled. He was pleased. Very, but he still hadn't decided whether he should say something. I mean, it was weird. He wasn't a hundred percent convinced there wasn't a tiny clear discharge from his left nipple after he got dried from the shower a second time. They were definitely larger, and he could hardly tell Marco he'd been tugging on them. He'd die.

Marco eyed him carefully and Darriel tried not to squirm. "How do you feel in other ways? Eating, sleeping?" He leaned back and stood. "In fact, let's check your weight. It's only been a few days since last time I checked but it won't hurt."

Darriel—reluctantly—got on the scales. He knew his jeans were slacker. Marco recorded his weight and took Darriel's arm, firmly guiding him to a chair. He sat down opposite him. "You've lost five pounds you can't afford to lose."

Darriel slumped. What could he say?

"Is there something you're concerned about?"

Darriel focused and realized he'd been so lost in his thoughts he hadn't said anything about Karina's weight. "No, they're doing great. Emmy's letting me sleep as well."

"I didn't mean with the girls." Marco arched an eyebrow.

"Ryker does that," Darriel said crossly. "And Zeke." He had no defenses around alphas and it wasn't fair.

Marco chuckled. "If you'd rather talk to Dr. G—"

"No," Darriel said hurriedly. "It's nothing really."

"It's enough of something to be bothering you."

Darriel chewed his lip. "I think the weight loss is post pregnancy," he said a little defiantly, knowing he was lying. "But my chest is a little weird."

Marco didn't react just gestured to his shirt. "Let's see."

Darriel unbuttoned his shirt slowly, very slowly. "I don't normally notice them. I mean, they're not a thing." He felt his face heating. "And it just seems to have been in the last few days. I wondered if I'd bruised them." Heat raced up his face and Darriel was so glad no one would notice. Or that the one person who would wasn't here. He slid his arm out of his shirt and wanted to close his eyes. He felt cool fingers press his skin and flinched.

"Does that hurt?" Marco asked.

Darriel squirmed. "A little."

"Well, I'll be damned," Marco said in surprise and Darriel looked down. A clear drop of liquid had formed on end of his nipple. He groaned. "They did that earlier as well."

Marco sat back and studied Darriel's face, then handed him a tissue. Darriel took it, wiped himself, and buttoned his shirt.

"There's something wrong isn't there?"

"Did you know men have milk ducts?"

Darriel gaped. "What?"

Marco nodded. "Human male breastfeeding is possible, but the hormone prolactin is needed plus some extra ducts that are present in female breasts not in male ones."

"But—"Darriel's protest didn't get anywhere. He had no idea what to say.

"Is there a likelihood you are pregnant?"

Darriel scowled. "I would never cheat."

"I didn't mean that," Marco said. "I actually meant with Zeke."

"But he's human," Darriel protested. "It's not possible." *And I'm not enough to make him come home.* There, he'd admitted it. If Zeke truly loved him, he wouldn't stay away.

"Josephine gave birth to a panther omega. I was always brought up knowing there's no such thing as an omega born to mixed parents, and I have no evidence to prove it either way. It may be a rumor to discourage mixed mating, but it's not impossible to believe that Zeke may have some shifter blood in him. Not enough to notice, but perhaps enough to cause this, especially in his mate."

Darriel looked down at himself as if he expected to see something. "But humans don't have mates."

Marco didn't reply, just stood and got out a small pack from the cupboard, handing it over. He nodded to the bathroom door. "Let's see."

Darriel took it in shaky hands. "But...it's not even two weeks. Will it work?"

"They're pretty accurate in humans these days and shifter hormones in omegas are a hundred times stronger than even female wolves. They have to be to operate two different sets of biology. The pregnancy, as you already know, is much shorter. The symptoms are more severe and start sooner. Have you noticed anything? Weird food cravings, nausea? Nausea might be the reason you have lost weight."

"I'm just not very hungry," he said a little pathetically. He knew why he didn't want to eat, and it wasn't nausea, or not because he might be pregnant.

Darriel went to the bathroom and peed on the stick. Afterwards he stood and stared at himself in the mirror. He didn't look at the test, just handed it back to Marco. He was probably in shock. And he definitely wasn't pregnant. This was absurd.

Marco looked down. "Congratulations."

Darriel blinked at him. "I've never known a wolf omega that can breastfeed." Which wasn't what he was going to say at all. In fact, he wasn't a hundred percent certain he wasn't going to be sick. *Pregnant?* Marco opened the small fridge and pulled out a bottle of water, handing it over. Maybe he'd turned green.

"I've heard of it in some shifter groups. I think some cat shifters can, but no, I've never heard of it in wolves, but it's incredible." Darriel gaped at him. He wouldn't call it incredible. He'd call it impossible.

*"I'm pregnant?"* It was more unbelievable than being able to breastfeed. "But why couldn't I feed the girls then?"

"I'm guessing whatever shifter genealogy is in Zeke is influencing this. We don't even understand really how we can exist as two separate beings, so the thought of your current pregnancy influencing something that's never happened to you before is hardly inconceivable. The main thing to remember is that in approximately four and a half months you're both going to have a baby."

Utter and total panic washed over Darriel like a tsunami. "I can't," he whispered. He didn't even know if Zeke was going to stay with him now. He'd told him he had his heart, but did he? He'd left. The whole thing with the omegas and the threats were messing him up. What if he decided Darriel was too much bother? "Please don't tell anyone."

Marco inclined his head. "So long as you don't put yourself or the baby at risk."

"What about doctor-patient confidentiality?"

Marco grinned. "You've been listening to Emmett. Firstly, I'm not a doctor, but I also have a sworn duty to my alpha. I will respect your confidence so long as it doesn't affect the pack. You know this," he added gently.

*And breaking into an omega compound will definitely affect the pack.*

"I just need a few days," Darriel said and stood. He needed longer than that but couldn't think of anything else to say.

"Don't forget the alphas will be able to hear the heartbeat soon anyway. Ryker might even be able to now," Marco reminded him. Darriel nodded. He knew that. They just needed to get through the next few days. Rescue Bodhi. Defeat a clan. Easy. It was just getting Zeke to come back to him that might be impossible.

# Chapter Thirteen

Z eke was going out of his mind. He missed Darriel so damned much he was ready just to walk into the Davies brothers' compound right that minute, but he had to make himself accessible, and he didn't dare annoy the clan. Regina was doing her best, but Ryker had confided there was a chance she was going to be asked to be on the shifter council. They needed someone like Regina in their corner, but to do that she needed to be beyond reproach and interfering with what seemed to be a human affair wouldn't help her cause. The shifter council had never interfered with inter-clan politics before, or the abuse of omegas. Zeke had no proof of who had held him, either. They could be rogues for all he knew.

He'd spent a long time on the phone with Ryker discussing the threat to Trina. Marco had been brought in, obviously, but while he was very protective of his sister there was nothing he could actually do. In fact, the thought that his brother or worse his mother might be responsible for not only the attack on Zeke, but also the threat to Trina was all kinds of wrong.

And he missed Darriel like his soul had been left behind. Zeke wasn't religious or even spiritual, but he felt the absence of Darriel in his heart like a living thing.

Darriel had asked him when he was coming home, and Zeke had wanted to go right then and there. He'd loved making Darriel come just by talking, but that had been five days ago, and they were heading nearly into nearly two weeks of being apart. He knew the Davies brothers were fucking with him. Just stringing it out. Work was the answer, though. Work had always been the answer.

But what if the question had changed? Did he really need to be at the office five days a week? He still had meetings, but so long as he had a laptop he could work from anywhere, and May was capable of running the day-to-day concerns for the charities. Both of them. Maybe he should promote her and get her an assistant?

Actually, that was a pretty good idea. The intercom light on his desk flashed and as if he had conjured her up, May informed him Dr. Deerman was here. He jumped up and went out to meet the doctor. He liked what he'd seen so far. Griffin had handled finding out about shifters with remarkable aplomb and he was helping Mo. Zeke had invited him to meet Max and see their lab. He put out his hand to shake and greet him. "Glad you could make it."

Griffin smiled, opened his mouth, then seemed to realize they weren't alone. "It's fine." Zeke assured him. "May is Max's twin sister and a bear shifter."

Griffin's eyes widened in shock, but he was too polite to say anything until they'd left. "So, body mass isn't a consideration then? That's even more incredible." He shot Zeke a wary look as they got in the elevator. "So long as we're not talking koalas."

"I'm sure you're very well aware that koalas aren't bears," Zeke chuckled. "But no, I mean a black bear. May tells me she is unusual in her family. Max isn't huge though. Not what you'd call a bear of a man." He grinned and directed Griffin down a corridor and into a large office. He would leave them to it in the lab but he wanted to do introductions first. Max wasn't a big guy at all, maybe five foot seven and slim. He had a very casual air about him except when he started talking about his research and then he got enthusiastic very quickly.

"I understand you are doing specific research," Griffin said curiously. "But Zeke was very cagey about its purpose." Zeke had gotten the okay from Ryker to explain about omegas and he was quite looking forward to Griffin's reaction.

Max nodded enthusiastically. "Specifically male omega pregnancy."

Griffin tilted his head as if he hadn't heard exactly what Max had said. Max was blissfully unaware he had said anything shocking, assuming with Griffin's presence it meant he knew. Griffin glanced at Zeke, his expression clearly intimating he had misunderstood or was being pranked.

Zeke took pity on him. "Yep. You heard correctly. Male omegas carry the internal organs of both sexes."

"That's impossible," Griffin said in astonishment.

"I'll leave you in Max's capable hands to explain, but I'm not joking. The research is to try and prevent problems. Babies are born fully developed at around five months, but as I'm sure you can guess, the window between viability and delivery is very small. Miscarriages even at almost full term are nearly always fatal. We're looking at getting some sort of incubators and Marco, while very good at his job, is a medic not a pediatrician and definitely not a neonatologist."

Max soon had the doctor discussing things Zeke didn't understand so he decided to leave them to it.

"So are you saying any male could get a male omega pregnant?" Griffin asked Max. They were both poring over a computer screen.

"Well, I couldn't," Zeke said flatly and turned to go. It had been a long time since he had his blood taken.

Max clicked some buttons. "Certain males possess a gene that enables osmosis in omegas. You see here, this is Mr. Coleman's results. All our human staff undertake these tests as a matter of course to establish baselines. He..." Max fell silent, and Zeke paused and turned back. Max was staring at the screen, and he glanced nervously at Zeke.

"What?" Zeke asked.

"I--."

"What?" Zeke asked testily.

"The pH is completely different to regular humans." Griffin pointed at something on the screen and Max swallowed. He turned to look at Zeke.

"I've never looked at your results specifically, sir. You had them done before I started here."

Zeke narrowed his eyes. "Spell it out."

"According to your tests you are capable of impregnating a male omega."

Zeke sat in his office and stared at his phone. *You are capable of impregnating a male omega.* But they had cycles, heats, or they did when triggered by a wolf. No, it was impossible. Darriel couldn't possibly be pregnant. But in the quiet of his office when everything was going so wrong in his world, he had an image of Darriel, his heavily pregnant belly carrying their child, and for a moment wished it was true. He toyed with his phone, the urge to hear Darriel's voice nearly overwhelming, but he worried in his current state he might blurt something out.

No, this discussion needed to be face to face and private.

He did speak to Darriel later as he had done every day, but it was a totally different conversation from the one they had when he had just gotten out of the shower, and not just because of the obvious, but because Darriel seemed tense. Although, so was Zeke, so he might easily be imagining little silences and guarded words where there were none.

The Davies brothers hadn't called and, disgusted with himself, he set off to his parking garage.

His phone rang just as he got in the car and he looked at the screen warily. *Unknown number.* Sickness washed over him, and his thumb hovered over the screen. He closed his eyes and pressed to accept. "Coleman."

"You decided to stop wasting our time?"

Zeke snapped his eyes open, almost giddy at the sound of Paxton Davies when he was worried it might be another. He'd been waiting for them, and they knew it. They were just fucking with him. It was time to turn the tables. "That's right." He paused. "I have to say, your proposal intrigued me."

There was a silence. Zeke knew his carefully chosen words weren't what the brothers were expecting, but then, Zeke had spent a lifetime doing the unexpected.

"Well then I guess we're both straight talkers." It was also a cautious reply. Zeke didn't laugh. He'd met plenty of snakes like Paxton Davies and he knew how to deal with them.

"Indeed," Zeke agreed. "Perhaps as we're both businessmen and truly understand the world of supply and demand, a meeting with less emotional individuals present would be beneficial to both of us." He could practically hear the rusty cogs straining to move in Paxton's fatuous brain.

"You want to meet us on your own?" He could hear the disbelief in Paxton's voice and continued to reel him in.

"I'm sure you're aware having individuals present who are not well-versed in financial dealings can be problematic." At the silence, Zeke wondered if he was being too clever but he was choosing his words carefully to portray the exact image he wanted. He was all but telling Paxton he was open to a "deal" and didn't want the shifters to be there. And he wasn't doing it in one-syllable words.

He heard sly laughter down the phone and rolled his eyes. "Sounds good to me."

"I'm not interested in standing in a muddy field, though," Zeke continued. "I understand discretion but we're not animals." Zeke winced. His grandfather would have been horrified at his lack of subtlety.

Paxton laughed again. "On your own, then."

He needed to get invited there. "I can arrange the meeting in one of my office suites, but I want to see the asset."

"I'm not coming to no offices. You meet us where we say."

"I would still need to see him."

Paxton scoffed. "Not a damaged hair on his head."

"Good," Zeke replied. "Protecting a mutually beneficial financial investment is good business sense and I only deal with people who understand that."

There was a silence. "You can come here."

"Agreed. Let me know a date and time." He clicked off not giving Paxton a chance to reply. He couldn't seem too eager. He breathed out a sigh and tossed his phone onto the other car seat and took a deep breath. It started ringing almost immediately and he tensed, then saw it was Marco. "Is everything okay?"

Marco was silent for a second. "This is none of my business except for pack welfare, and because I'm a medic."

A chill swept over Zeke. "What is it?"

"Darriel's not doing too good. I have no idea how human/shifter mating affects the bond but in my previous experience it's not the same as shifter to shifter. However, your continued absence is affecting him. He's not even going to Ryker for comfort, and with the doubled security patrols, my alpha hasn't noticed he needs him."

"Ryker?" Zeke sputtered, real and very visceral jealousy taking a knife to his heart.

"Some omegas can successfully take comfort from their alpha in the absence of their mate. I suggest you make sure it isn't necessary." Marco clicked off.

In an hour he was on his way back up the mountain in his car, not even stopping to contact his pilot, and not giving a flying fuck about the clan either. He had no idea exactly what Marco meant. He knew

—absolutely knew—that Ryker wouldn't cheat on Emmett, but the thought of Darriel turning to anyone else for comfort made him want to rip something apart with his bare hands. He should be the one offering comfort. *But you haven't been there, dumbass.*

He knew the scouts would have seen him pass the bottom gate even though he couldn't see them, and as he started the climb up to the pack house, he thought again about his reaction to the phone call, as well as about how to rescue Bodhi. He would have to set up a fictitious buyer, which was easy. The real problem was how to get rid of the threat to Zeke's family. He'd spoken to Ryker nearly every day and they were no further along, but he could only do this one step at a time, and they couldn't firm any plans until they had a date and time.

He pulled up outside the pack house, dragged himself out of the car with his case, but didn't take so much as one step before the main door was opened and a whirlwind ran down the steps. He dropped his case and opened his arms just in time to get an armful of Darriel. He squeezed his eyes tight and shamelessly clung on. Why had he stayed away so damn long?

Because he'd been terrified. Terrified his presence put Darriel in danger. He met Darriel's lips and practically mauled them. Heat shot through him. He held him in his arms easily, like he belonged. He broke off for air, Darriel still held him as if afraid to let him go. Zeke raked his gaze up and down his beautiful man. Thinner. He had on a bulky sweater, but Zeke could practically feel his ribs. He pulled him close again and tucked Darriel's head under his chin. "I'm sorry."

Darriel slid his head up so he could see Zeke's face. "Sorry for what?" Suspicion slid into his words.

"Because I shouldn't have stayed away." He smoother Darriel's hair away from his face where the wind had picked it up. "I thought I was keeping you safe."

Tears sprang to Darriel's eyes. "I'm safe with you."

Zeke nodded, turned to his car, and got out his bag all the while keeping his other hand on Darriel's. "I haven't eaten, do you think Dinah would mind if I raided her kitchen?" He wasn't especially hungry, but he was going to make damn certain Darriel ate something. If he was pregnant— Zeke swallowed and managed to keep quiet as they walked in. The urge to wake Marco and demand Darriel have an examination was nearly overpowering. He wasn't going to let him out of his sight until he'd spoken to Marco and Ryker. "Where are the girls?"

"Asleep. Safe. Chrissy came in to tell me you were on your way when the scouts reported in. She's staying with them until we get there."

"I want you to move into my suite," Zeke said.

Darriel's eyes lit up. "You do?"

Zeke smiled and opened the door and they walked into the kitchen. "I don't want to sleep separately, but it's not fair of me to go to the omega side."

Dinah straightened up from the stove and beamed at them. "I just put some of the chicken I made this afternoon to warm. It will be ready in fifteen minutes. I'll go keep Chrissy company. No rush." She smiled and left.

Zeke thanked her gratefully and pulled Darriel to a chair. He wanted a good look at him.

"Tell me what's been happening."

Darriel tipped his head in confusion. "I was going to ask you that."

Zeke poked him in the ribs. "You've lost weight." Darriel ducked his head immediately. "Sweetheart," Zeke said gently, lifting his chin with his finger. "I'm sorry I left. I have things to do. This business with Bodhi and the clan isn't resolved, and I have to make sure everyone's safe."

"But you don't need to do it on your own."

Zeke shook his head. "I'm going to meet the Davies brothers soon. They pose no threat to me. They're just a couple of bullies." *With guns.* But Zeke didn't say that. Darriel didn't need any extra worries.

"How are you feeling?" Which was as close as he dared get to what he really wanted to know. *Are you pregnant* wasn't an easy question to ask. He almost laughed at the understatement. He was glad Darriel seemed not to demand more than his physical presence.

"I missed you," Darriel admitted, and Zeke berated himself. He knew how the absence of a mate could affect shifters and—whoa—*a mate?* He was human. But...Max had told him he was capable of getting Darriel pregnant. He was so out of his depth he felt like a freshman that had just been noticed by a cheerleader. *Or the quarterback?*

*Fuck.*

Was he going to have to pry the information out of Darriel? *Yes.* Darriel didn't trust him, and he didn't blame him. He was, for all intents and purposes, a human. A rich human. A bossy human. He could be—*was*—intimidating. Except he loved this wolf omega with every beat of his heart. Had done for weeks. The first time he had visited Mills River and Darriel had been lying there, so small in that huge bed, Zeke had desperately wanted to gather him in his arms and promise him it would be okay. Falling in love had been easy. Keeping him safe wasn't as simple.

Their food was ready and Darriel dished it out. Zeke couldn't have cared less what he ate, just that Darriel did. And he did. He seemed to hoover every crumb. It made Zeke feel twelve feet tall, which was all kinds of ridiculous. They cleared away the dishes and went to Darriel's room. Chrissy and Dinah had gotten the girls' stuff ready, or what they would need for tomorrow anyway, so Dinah had obviously heard what he'd said when they came in. He met Chrissy's eyes and smiled his gratitude. Chrissy and Dinah wished them both a good night. They trundled both cots to Zeke's room as quietly as they could.

And then they were alone.

Zeke saw Darriel quickly cover the yawn that had taken him by surprise and he smiled. He undressed and got ready for bed, noticing Darriel had kept his baggy T-shirt on. When he took Darriel in his arms and didn't attempt anything other than a heartfelt kiss, Darriel didn't seem disappointed. He was too busy snuggling, and Zeke didn't need to do anything other than hold him safe. Zeke was a very lucky man, and his last thought before he closed his eyes was to make sure this was what he did—or could do—every day for the rest of his life.

# Chapter Fourteen

Darriel woke to the sight of Zeke, dressed, holding Emmy and his heart melted. Zeke was apparently warming to his theme of what the girls were going to do when they were older. "Dartmouth is good. It's where I went, and it has a smaller vibe. You have to put in the work though." He kissed her forehead and picked up the warmed bottle of milk, then seemed to notice Darriel was watching him. He flushed and nodded to Karina. "Sleeping beauty is still catching zees."

"What were you telling her?" Darriel asked as he got up and went to see to Karina. Zeke grinned sheepishly.

"Of course, it'll depend on her interests. Lots of good schools not too far away, or at least on the east coast. I was thinking maybe this shifter council ought to provide safe temporary packs."

"Huh?" Darriel paused.

"Well, they're going to need somewhere safe to shift, aren't they? We could get a register of alphas willing to provide safe spaces when there isn't time for her to visit home."

Darriel picked up Karina to change her diaper. "You're serious, aren't you?" He'd thought...what? That Zeke was teasing? No, but he hadn't thought it through. It was more of a pipe dream. But was it? Wasn't this why he wanted to help rescue Bodhi? Or try?

Zeke walked over to the bed and casually added. "I have to go see Ryker as soon as she's done."

Darriel met his gaze, and he knew. His heart thumped. "Why?"

"The Davies brothers want to meet this afternoon."

Darriel didn't know what to say, but Ryker and Chrissy would be fierce. "Be careful. Will you need me?" Zeke smiled.

"Always. But not for this," he added.

He stood rubbing Emmy's back until she burped like a sailor. He chuckled and settled her in the stroller with her favorite rattle then walked over to Darriel, cupping his cheek. "We didn't have time to talk about much, but let's get this done and then we will." He brushed his lips across Darriel's and Darriel's toes curled. He'd hoped to be woken in a different way this morning.

"Later," Zeke murmured, obviously reading his mind. He slid a finger down Darriel's neck and down under his T-shirt. Darriel gasped, shuddering, and closed his eyes on the wondrous sensation of Zeke's finger sliding over his pecs. About the same time as realization dawned, closely followed by blind panic, Zeke paused. Darriel jerked back and opened his eyes. Zeke was staring at his T-shirt and the damp stain on the front of it. Darriel closed his eyes in utter horror, but he felt Zeke's finger leave his chest and hook under his chin, tilting it up gently. "Darriel?"

Darriel whimpered but opened his eyes and his gaze was immediately trapped by the intensity of the blue-gray ones staring at him. He opened his mouth but closed it again. Darriel glanced down. "Take your shirt off," Zeke ordered.

He couldn't breathe but he still obeyed his alpha. He didn't look, knowing what Zeke would see. His pecs swollen, dark nipples and the clear fluid leaking out of both of them. Zeke didn't say a word, just trailed a finger lightly across his nipple. Darriel shivered, the touch hardening his cock so quickly, for a second he was afraid he would shoot. He pressed a hand over his groin, then looked back up to see Zeke focused on his hand. Then Zeke laid another hand on his pecs, cupping them. "Do they hurt?" He almost whispered the words.

Darriel shook his head. Zeke brushed his thumb over Darriel's nipples, and another bead of liquid appeared. Zeke's eyes met his, then with utter and complete focus he drew his thumb back and lifted it to his mouth, pushing it between his lips and licking the fluid. Another wave of utter lust swept over Darriel, and he gasped, pushing his fist down hard on his groin. "I'm—" He swallowed.

"Look at me," Zeke commanded and Darriel's head shot up, his gaze pinned by the intensity in those dark eyes. Holding his gaze, Zeke never faltered. He cupped each of Darriel's breasts and dragged his thumbs over them both. Darriel cried out, arching and pushing into his hands. "Let go," he demanded but it was unnecessary. Darriel came, the touch to his nipples sending a one-way explosive current to his cock. When he opened them again, trembling and gasping from the potency, Zeke sank to his knees and gathered him in his arms.

Darriel was shivering but not from cold, and for a glorious moment reveled in the strong arms holding him and just let himself be. After a few seconds he tried to pull back and Zeke let him move but didn't get up. "Your shirt," Darriel whispered, seeing the damp spot.

Zeke glanced down in bemusement, but fresh embarrassment rolled over Darriel. He was sticky. He'd come in his shorts and, and... He took a hurried gulp.

"Has Marco seen them?"

Darriel froze. He felt his heart—just calming from his orgasm—begin to pound. "Yesterday."

Zeke nodded and took both his hands in his. "Are you pregnant?"

Tears sprang to Darriel's eyes and without saying a word, Zeke pulled him back against him. "Your shirt," Darriel gasped again, and Zeke answered him by peppering kisses on his head.

"Fuck the shirt." Which made Darriel want to laugh because he'd never heard Zeke swear. Zeke pushed him back a little until they were looking at each other. "What? I mean, is this something to do with you being pregnant. Has it happened before?"

"Why aren't you surprised?" Darriel asked, bewildered.

"Because by an incredible coincidence, I took Griffin to the lab yesterday to see the set-up. Ryker said I was okay to tell him about male omegas and then in an effort to prove it was impossible for me to get you pregnant, Max pulled my blood and sperm results up. Bearing in mind I had these done just as a base line years ago when we were just setting things up. At that time, our focus wasn't on male pregnancy, so no one was looking at the results for that."

"But you can?" Darriel said in awe.

Zeke huffed. "It's to be hoped so, or this would be a very different conversation." He tilted his head and studied Darriel. "What about your pecs, breasts, whatever you want to call them?"

"I went to Marco for the girls' check yesterday and I thought—" Darriel squirmed. "I thought because I'd been tugging on them when we—" Zeke grinned.

"You thought you'd hurt yourself?"

"I didn't know," Darriel hissed. "I didn't know it was even possible and it definitely didn't happen before. Marco says whatever super sperm you've got going on caused it."

Zeke's grin was wicked and Darriel almost rolled his eyes. He was such an alpha. Zeke got to his feet and glanced at his phone then over to the sleeping babies. "I have to go." He smirked again. "And you need a shower."

Darriel sobered, humor vanishing. Zeke bent and kissed him again but before Darriel could respond he stepped back. "I'll see you after the meeting." And then he was gone.

Darriel grabbed a quick shower, and then he pushed the girls in the stroller toward the kitchen. He knew if Zeke was with Ryker, Emmett would be waiting for him. He met Emmet's gaze as he walked in and went straight to their corner. Dinah wasn't there but there were a few others grabbing coffee.

Emmett glanced down at his phone and huffed. "Trina's coming this afternoon, which means the claw will be here. This place will be more locked down than Fort Knox."

"This afternoon?" He'd thought it was tomorrow.

Emmett nodded. "Regina's bringing her to visit with Marco and she needs to see Ryker. She just texted me, really excited."

Darriel frowned. "But isn't the meeting with the Davies brothers happening this afternoon?"

Emmett flushed.

"What?" Darriel's pulse picked up.

"I might have overheard him talking to Zeke this morning."

*"And?"*

"Zeke's going on his own."

Darriel gaped. "He can't. What if—" He couldn't even think about the what ifs.

"I think Zeke's hoping to get taken to the compound. They wouldn't let him anywhere near if he wasn't on his own."

"And Ryker's letting him?" Darriel hissed but as soon as he said it, he knew it wasn't like that. No one "let" Zeke do anything.

"This is to rescue Bodhi and the others?" Darriel frowned. "This sounds like a bad idea. What can Zeke do on his own? Hasn't Ryker told you what's going on?"

Emmett shot him a desperate look. "He *always* talks to me. Tells me stuff, and I know what I can share and what I can't. The fact he's not is worrying me."

Darriel sat. "What do we know?"

Emmett blew out a breath. "That we're rescuing the omegas including Bodhi."

"The Davies brothers bought omegas from Riggs because they're convinced shifters are going to take over the world and want their own personal army." Darriel paused. "Why is Zeke going?"

"What do you mean?"

"I mean that Ryker always does the rescues. Leaving it to Zeke makes no sense. I don't buy that it's because they're human," Darriel said slowly, a million thoughts rushing through his head. He sat up suddenly. "That's impossible. How do they know Zeke is human? They're not shifters. They can't tell."

"I have no idea," Emmett said. "But you're right about them not knowing he's human unless Bodhi told them. It hadn't occurred to me but everything about this is wrong."

"I saw them, they were quite happy to talk to Ryker."

"What else—" Emmett cut his words off. "This can't possibly be to do with the clan."

"I agree. It makes no sense. Except...why won't they say? You said Ryker isn't telling you, which says to me this is a big deal." Darriel flushed. "I didn't mean that saving omegas—" Emmett waved a hand.

"I agree. But how on earth could a mixed-breed omega have anything to do with a clan?"

"Do you think Trina might know?"

They both turned at the sound of a car. Two cars. Regina's Mercedes and the second car carrying her claw. Eight massive guys got out of both cars and looked around surreptitiously before opening the back doors. Darriel frowned. That was different. Because Trina was here?

"Did that seem over the top to you?"

Emmett nodded. "Yes. There's something going on. We need to get Trina on her own."

Darriel clasped the stroller. "I'm going to feed the twins. Didn't you say Trina wanted to do that?"

Emmett grinned in understanding. Darriel knew Trina had said nothing of the sort but either she'd be too polite to call Emmett out or she'd be intrigued enough to go with it. Darriel pushed the stroller into his room and sure enough maybe not even five minutes had gone by before Emmett appeared with Trina.

She gazed at the stroller. "They're asleep. You said they were going to be fed and you needed an extra pair of hands." She narrowed her eyes. "What?"

Emmett grinned, looped her arm with his, and dragged her to sit on Darriel's bed. "What's going on?"

Trina went exceptionally still. "What do you mean?"

Emmett glanced at Darriel. "Oh, she's good. She's even got the raised eyebrow down pat."

Trina tried to stand but Emmett clung on.

"Zeke's going to get himself killed and I love him." It came out in a desperate rush, and it was the only thing Darriel could think to say.

Trina's eyes widened and her shoulders sagged. "I don't know for sure and that's kind of freaky."

"Why?" Emmett asked.

"Because Regina's, like, brutally honest. The good and the bad. She says knowledge is power. The one universal currency, and for the first time, I've been reduced to sneaking around." Emmett elbowed her gently.

"I knew we could rely on you."

"What do you know?" Darriel pressed.

She glanced back at the door to make sure it was shut. "You can't tell."

"Not unless we have to, to save Zeke's life," Darriel countered, which made Trina nod once in agreement.

"Have you ever read Rudyard Kipling?"

Emmett barked out a laugh. "Jungle Book?"

"I've never read it, but I know of it," Darriel said slowly. "Why?"

"Because according to shifter mythology Bagheera was a panther shifter. I learned that in school."

Darriel glanced at Emmett. "Okay." He had no idea what that had to do with anything. She shot another nervous glance to the door and all three huddled around, dropping their voices. "I heard Regina on the phone with Ryker. She was on her cell phone and in the bedroom. I wasn't supposed to be in there and as soon as she saw me, she shut up, but I heard her say they had to try and contact the Khan."

Darriel and Emmett looked blankly at each other. "The Khan?" Emmett repeated. "What...*no*." He shook his head as if answering his own question. "In the film, book, whatever. Are you talking about the *tiger*?"

"Shere Khan?" Darriel asked, and they both hushed him immediately.

Emmett sat back. "You're going to tell me he was a tiger shifter."

She nodded. "Like I said, I learned this in school, but they only teach it to us because of panther mythology. If Bagheera was a raccoon, they wouldn't care."

Darriel nearly asked if there were raccoon shifters, but that was hardly the point. "But what has that got to do with anything?"

Trina wriggled a little and smiled, obviously warming to her story. "So, tiger shifters are supposed to be extinct, yes?"

Darriel shrugged. He'd honestly never thought about it.

"Yes," Emmett said confidently.

"Well, the name for a tiger pack is a khan, but the alpha is also called *the* Khan."

"And you think that's what you heard Regina say?" Darriel asked.

"I *know* that's what she said," Trina said. "I just don't know what it has to do with anything."

"How big a deal is it if they find this Khan?" Emmett asked slowly.

Trina scoffed. "Are you kidding me?"

"Yes, of course I am," Emmett answered dryly, and Trina had the grace to look apologetic.

"Sorry. But yes, it's a huge deal. Legend says the Khan is like the boss of all the shifters. Like they had to do what he said all the time."

Emmett chuckled. "Sorry, but I can't see Gran doing anything other than what she wants."

"I agree," Trina said. "Except she said it almost *reverently*. I've never heard her talk like that."

"But even if this is true, what has it got to do with a mixed-breed omega, a group of humans, and a clan?"

"And Zeke," Darriel pointed out.

"And Dad," Emmett agreed.

Trina huffed. "I don't know."

Darriel laughed. "You know what would be so funny but at the same time really wouldn't be?" Emmett and Trina both looked at him. He leaned forward. "That Bodhi is a long-lost tiger shifter." He smiled. It wasn't funny. It was completely *ridiculous*.

"Who's Bodhi?" Trina asked carefully.

"He's one of the omegas we're trying to rescue from the human dipwads," Emmett said, and raised his head to shoot Darriel an ironic smile. Like they were sharing a joke. But even as Emmett met Darriel's gaze they both sobered.

They stared at each other and it all—everything, every weird reaction from Ryker, Regina, and Zeke suddenly made perfect sense.

"Shit," Emmett said eloquently. "What if he isn't just a tiger shifter?"

Darriel stared at the other two. "I can't let Zeke go on his own. I don't understand what's going on. If Bodhi is this Khan, then the fact that Regina and Ryker aren't going seems so unbelievable it's disturbing."

Trina was silent for a moment. Quiet. They both waited, knowing she was debating saying something else. "What if someone else knows about Bodhi?"

"Well Chrissy—" Darriel started, but Trina waved a dismissive hand at him.

"No. I was thinking why Zeke." She paused, as if waiting for Darriel and Emmett to catch up. "What just happened to Zeke?"

Darriel gasped. "This has something to do with—" He faltered. He'd been going to say "your mom" but that sounded so wrong.

"My murderous, power hungry family?" Trina said lightly, but they could both see the hurt that glinted in her eyes. Emmett took her hand immediately.

"It makes sense," Emmett acknowledged. "They tried to get Trina because she represents control of the western clans. Control some people don't want to give up."

"Whereas Bodhi might be even more powerful," Darriel said quietly. "Why worry about just controlling panthers when you can take over the world?"

"I know Regina has withdrawn a little, even from the claw."

"Withdrawn?" Darriel echoed in disbelief. "With your entrance?"

Trina smirked. "Right? But no, I mean she always had a very tight-knit inner circle of protection. The claw is easily twenty-five guys, but Hansa, Asheel, Tam, and Loren were the four that always went in her car with her. The last few days, she's been changing things up. The guys won't say a word, but I think they're confused. And maybe a little hurt," she added.

"I never considered this," Emmett said carefully. "But how did they know where you were?"

Trina's eyes narrowed. "You think someone told them?"

"It makes sense," Darriel said. "And that someone either had to be from here or from the claw."

"So," Emmett counted off on his fingers. "Bodhi might be very powerful and for the same reasons they tried to take you, they're now going for a bigger prize." He chewed his cheek a moment. "I still don't see why Dad."

Trina held his gaze. "They did a lot to him, Emmett. What if—"

"He promised," Darriel whispered, tears springing to his eyes.

"Promised what?" Emmett asked.

"He promised to help them get Trina." Emmett's reared back, utter horror on his face.

"No. How can you possibly say that?"

Darriel reached out and grabbed his hand. "No, listen to me. I said he told them he would so they would let him go. I know Ryker knows this."

"So, you're thinking this is a big set up?" Trina said cautiously.

"That they're trying to fool the clan into thinking he's getting Bodhi for him but really he isn't. And that Ryker and Regina know and that's the plan."

"It's the only thing that makes any sense at all," Darriel said. "We need to be ready. An omega is the only one that could convince Bodhi, and it has to be me." He wasn't about to let Zeke do this on his own. Not ever again.

"Get in where?" Trina said doubtfully.

"Their compound. I can be convincing. I knew the shifter that dealt with them before. They'll let me in."

He saw the uneasy look Trina sent Emmett. "I'm not doubting you want to help, but what if you being there compromises everything?"

"You didn't see Bodhi. Alphas terrify him. I was the only one he even made eye contact with. How is Zeke going to persuade him to leave?"

"Okay, but I'm not waiting around up here. You go and I'm going to make Loren take me to help."

"You can't," Emmett gasped in a horrified voice. "He'll tell Regina."

"Actually," Trina said. "I don't think he will. I told you those four were hurt. They can tell she's keeping something from them and while I understand, any of the claw would lay down their lives for her in a heartbeat with no hesitation. Last week Regina said I had to start thinking about my own claw. Like an inner circle. I didn't mention it to Regina, but I asked Loren if he would become my Dion."

"Your what?" Emmett asked.

Trina slapped Emmett's arm. "You're half panther-shifter. You really should know your history," she scolded.

"What's a Dion?" Darriel asked.

"It's like a right-hand man, to use a human term. After the Greek God Dionysus, who favored panthers. Wolves would say beta commander or maybe enforcer." She shrugged. "It varies."

"Like Red," Darriel agreed.

"You think if you told him he wouldn't go straight to Gran?"

Trina shook her head. "He agreed and insisted we tell Regina and she agreed, which means his first loyalty now is to me, not her. And trust me, those guys don't mess around."

An hour later, all the alphas walked into the kitchen where they were sitting with Kai. Darriel thought almost abstractedly how good they looked and then he saw his alpha, and he melted. He was using stuffed tissues under a tight tank top topped off by a baggy sweater, but he needed something better. He swore that just seeing Zeke stride confidently into the room made him leak. In more than one place.

Zeke immediately met his gaze. The smile was full of lazy promises. "Eww," Emmett complained, and covered his eyes. "I did not need to see that from my dad." But then Ryker appeared and suddenly Emmett didn't care. Kai snickered. They felt awful not sharing what Trina had confided but it wasn't fair to expect Kai not to say something this important to Marco. Kai still thought they were going to try and rescue the omegas though.

"Marco can see us now." Darriel nodded, expecting nothing less. And it wasn't like he didn't believe him; Zeke being Zeke, he would want every detail...in triplicate. Kai just took the stroller handles and moved it nearer to him. Darriel shot him a grateful glance. They both walked into the clinic and sat down next to Marco who was waiting for them.

"I found out yesterday I am capable of impregnating an omega." As an opening, Darriel thought, it was so typically Zeke. No bullshit.

Marco nodded and sat back. "Are you two mated?"

"Surely that's not possible between a human and a shifter in the sense you mean," Zeke answered carefully.

"And yet, neither is a male omega pregnancy." Zeke inclined his head as if he was agreeing and Marco turned to Darriel. "How are you feeling?"

Darriel hated having both sets of intense eyes on him, but for once he could answer honestly. "Good. I've been hungrier today, and no problems with eating." Kai had been pretty shocked when he'd asked for and eaten a second breakfast.

Zeke smiled and nudged him. "That's great."

Marco nodded. "And yesterday? What did you eat?"

Darriel squirmed. "I had breakfast," he mumbled.

"No you didn't," Marco said gently. "I have it on good authority that you had a single piece of ham then pushed the rest around your plate."

"I had a big supper," Darriel argued almost defiantly.

Marco raised his eyebrows. "And what do those three meals have in common?"

Darriel shrugged. Why the twenty questions? He ate when he was hungry.

"My presence," Zeke said flatly. Darriel turned to Zeke in mild annoyance. So, he was happier when Zeke was there. *Duh.* "But that's impossible," Zeke said slowly.

"And we all thought a human getting an omega pregnant was as well. He's gone downhill so fast in your absence you understand why I had to call you."

Darriel stilled. He could practically feel every drop of happiness drain from him like Marco had suddenly pulled a plug. He stared at Marco. "You called him." Zeke hadn't returned because he'd been unable to stay away from Darriel. He'd returned because Marco had *summoned* him. Because Darriel wasn't a draw all on his own. He stood. On his feet without being conscious of the move.

Marco winced visibly. "I was worried." But Darriel ignored him. He walked to the door as if in a daze.

"Darriel?" Zeke grabbed his arm. "Sweetheart, that's not why I came back."

Darriel met his gaze. "Isn't it? Can you swear on Josie's life that Marco's call didn't make you get in the car? That if he hadn't said anything you wouldn't still be in Asheville?"

Zeke opened his mouth then swallowed his words. He tried again. "That's not what happened."

"Would you have come back last night if Marco hadn't called you?" He held his breath, but the resignation he saw in Zeke's eyes told him the answer without him saying a word. He yanked his arm from Zeke's grasp. "Let me go." He didn't look back as he ran from the room.

# Chapter Fifteen

Darriel showed up for lunch. He fed the girls. He talked. He smiled. He pushed his food around and he didn't so much as look in Zeke's direction. He was also well aware that it was only because things were so crazy that he was getting away with it. He was willing to bet it was the first Thanksgiving dinner Regina had attended with nearly forty people all sitting on picnic- style benches. That was when Regina wasn't being charmed by Dr. Darling who was doing his best to snag her attention in between all the kids wanting them to look at this picture, or that fancy stone they'd dug out of the yard. He was good though. He didn't once get tired of the constant questions. He saw Regina look at the doctor a couple of times when he wasn't watching, and her lips twitched.

Thankfully it had been so busy with so many people, no one noticed Darriel not eating much.

"You need more than that."

Darriel's hand stilled and deliberately he put his fork down before he looked up, and every bit of defiance and anger drained away at the hurt in Zeke's eyes. "I'm not hungry."

He wished he was. Darriel leaned over to whisper a promise to eat later when Zeke's phone rang. He shot Darriel an apologetic glance and answered it, making sure he walked a good distance away from all the shifter hearing in the room. Darriel glanced at Emmett. They still didn't know what to do. He turned to look at Zeke and saw him seeming to clip one-word answers into the phone. He wasn't the only one watching him, either. Even though they were trying not to be obvious Ryker, Chrissy, and Regina kept their eyes on him.

His attention was caught when Zeke pushed his phone into his pocket and gave a barely perceptible nod to Ryker.

Darriel was on his feet before he'd even thought about it and wrapping his arms around him seconds later. Zeke didn't protest, just held on and kissed the top of Darriel's head where it was pressed against Zeke's chest. "I have to deal with something. I have to duck out of lunch."

For a very long second Darriel didn't trust himself to speak. "Problem?" he said quietly, desperately wanting him to scream at him to be careful.

"Work, sorry. But I'll be back." And as if it was a promise, he took Darriel's chin in his thumb and forefinger and tipped his face up. Their lips met hungrily, and not for the first time, Darriel felt devoured. The catcalls and whistling from the table made them break apart.

"You mean the world to me," Zeke said softly. "Please believe me." Darriel clung on tight until he felt Zeke stepping back.

"I might go and have a nap," Darriel said and yawned. "Then I can be awake for when you get back."

"Why don't you ask Charles to keep the girls so you can get some proper sleep?"

Darriel smiled weakly. "Because they're my responsibility and I ask them enough." Zeke kissed him on the nose.

"Try and rest." Darriel forced himself to take a step away but Zeke caught his arm and pulled him back. "I didn't just come here last night because of Marco. I love you and the thought of anything happening to you breaks me."

Darriel practically flung himself at Zeke again, kissed him until he needed oxygen, gasped out he loved him and he'd better be safe, then turned and hurried back to the table just as Ryker followed Zeke outside. Darriel caught Emmett's gaze and Emmett stood, nodding at the strollers and to Kai. In another couple of seconds Emmett let himself into Darriel's room. Darriel was pulling one of his old sweaters on. "You have to distract them. Zeke's leaving now."

"He's going to see you in the car," Emmett hissed.

"I'm getting in the trunk, but you have to distract them." Emmett stood, obviously completely undecided. "He's not going on his own."

Emmett grabbed Darriel and hugged him. "Be careful." Darriel nodded and dropped his phone inside his shirt then rushed out of the room, but instead of heading to the kitchen he slipped down the corridor and out of the side door, staying out of sight. Zeke and Ryker were standing by Zeke's truck talking urgently. Zeke took a step back towards his car and Darriel's breath hitched.

Then Emmett yelled at the top of his voice. "Panther." He pointed to the trees and Ryker took off, at least five claw following him. Zeke ran to the edge of the clearing and for a moment as everyone streamed out of the house it was bedlam. Chrissy and Red followed Ryker half shifted and Fox yelled at everyone else to get inside. Darriel ran and managed to get the trunk open before turning to check that he hadn't been seen, only to come face to face with TJ's astonished gaze. TJ just shook his head and slammed the trunk quickly before anyone noticed. Refusing to let frustrated tears fall, Darriel whirled around and ran back to his room.

He'd been so close. So damn close. Now Zeke was on his own and Darriel didn't know what to do. He kicked out at the table in utter frustration, then whirled around at the sound of a knock on the door.

He yanked it open, and TJ gazed at him. "I haven't told my alpha and you have precisely five minutes to convince me why I shouldn't."

Darriel slumped. "I just didn't want him to leave without me."

"That's crap and you know it. Maybe I should go ask Ryker to fetch Emmett, because if you're up to something I'm pretty sure he knows what it is."

"No," Darriel blurted out. He knew things had been strained between Ryker and Emmett because of the whole secrecy thing. He wasn't going to make it worse.

TJ sighed. "Look, I feel bad enough that I've let Ryker down as it is with Ginny being sick. Her dad's a nightmare and I haven't been pulling my weight around here because of it. Then there's losing my job and having to take more time off. Too much. If Ryker hadn't helped, I have no idea what I would have done. If there's something going on let me *do something*. I owe my alpha big time."

Darriel studied him. He knew they were having financial problems. Ginny was a mixed-breed shifter and her dad was human and slowly developing dementia. He knew it made everything a hundred times harder. Emmett was doing what he could and Darriel was sorry he hadn't been able to help.

"If I tell you it has to stay a secret."

TJ looked appalled. "Not from my alpha."

"He knows," Darriel said, thinking about a similar declaration from Marco, and how loyal the wolves were to Ryker because he was a good alpha and an even better man. TJ was just trying to raise a family. The thought made him rest his hands on his flat belly.

"Knows what?"

So Darriel told him about the omega rescue. "He's on his way there alone because one of the omegas is so terrified of alphas, he won't go near them. Zeke's hoping because he's a human he will, but I know something's going to go wrong and the omega knows me. Zeke is pretending to buy them." Which wasn't exactly true, but it was all he dared admit.

"How many altogether?" TJ asked.

"Maybe a dozen or so," Darriel hedged.

"But we always do the rescues together as a team. We're used to idiots with guns. We got Marco back. I don't get it. It's bad if we have one omega that's scared but we're used to this. It's happened tons of times." His phone rang and he answered it. Darriel held his breath.

It was Chrissy. He could hear her voice. "Got a job. I need you to follow Fox with the rescue truck. Fox is taking the bus."

TJ frowned. "We need two?" Then he shot an exasperated glance at Darriel. "We're bringing someone back?"

"Yes," Chrissy confirmed. "I'm texting you the address now. When you get a half mile away pull up and check in. Don't let the truck be seen."

"Okay." He agreed and pushed his phone in his pocket.

"Well, you're okay then. He's not going on his own."

"Take me with you," Darriel begged. Zeke was going on his own and Darriel was convinced he was going to get killed. There was no way the clan would leave him alive. The fact that the others were following didn't help. "I'm an omega. I can get in there. You guys can't."

TJ huffed and all but patted him on his head. "We've done a ton of these. Not sure why Zeke went unless it's because the fuckers are human, but we'll get him, don't worry."

"You don't understand," Darriel said helplessly.

"What don't I understand?"

"Because there's an omega there that's really rare. Marco's clan wants him badly and they've threatened to hurt Emmett and Josie if Zeke doesn't agree to go on his own and get him."

"What sort of shifter?" TJ asked doubtfully.

Darriel hesitated. "A tiger."

TJ shrugged. "Well, it's cool if they're not extinct, but there's no way a panther clan is interested." He patted Darriel's shoulder again like he was a child and Darriel snapped.

"They think he's the Khan," Darriel burst out. "The heir."

TJ gaped. "You've got to be kidding me. That's real?" Darriel nodded. "Well, no wonder they want him." He sighed. "Ryker's gonna fucking kill me."

Hope stabbed at Darriel. "You'll take me?"

"Be ready at the side door but I'm not promising I'm just going to let you go." He paused, seeming to think. "I'll get you close. If I think he needs help and you're the only one that can, then I'll let you. I'll drive the truck around. Get in and lie on the floor, pull the blanket over you. As soon as we clear the bottom gates, I'll pull over so you can hide better.

Darriel waited until TJ had gone then did as he was told. He was ready when the truck pulled up and he jumped in and got on the floor. He knew TJ would have to drive past the front of the pack house and needed him out of sight in case he was stopped by anyone. After a very uncomfortable ride he felt the wheels hit smooth road and heard TJ signal and pull over. He got out and came around to the side door, helping Darriel to his feet and to step out. "The ride's a little comfier from now on," he said apologetically. "Jump in the back. I'll just move the medical equipment." Darriel hopped in. TJ hesitated then pulled a box toward him, opening it. He looked up. "I'd better get some stuff ready up front. I know this is shit but sometimes we have to sedate the omegas. It's light, but we can't have them screaming while we get them out, especially if we don't want to alert anyone." Darriel nodded and glanced out of the window nervously. There weren't any cars anywhere. "Hold this?"

Darriel turned back and held out his hand but before he could react, TJ grabbed his wrist, yanked his arm forward and stuck a needle in him. He let go almost immediately. Panic washed over Darriel. "What did you do? What was that?" He scrambled forward but TJ moved even quicker and hopped in, effectively blocking Darriel's escape.

"Let me go," he yelled and lunged for the door. TJ caught his arms and pinned them. He moved behind him pulling Darriel back so his legs couldn't kick out either.

"Hush, I'm sorry."

"Sorry for what?" Darriel struggled but TJ was much stronger.

"Just relax," TJ murmured.

"Relax?" Darriel spat out. "Are you insane?"

"No," TJ said sadly. "That'd be Ginny's dad, who owes over a hundred thousand dollars in gambling debts."

"What did you do?" He had to try and do something. Stall?

"In trying to sort it out, I managed to dig us in deeper." He swallowed nervously. "I told someone something and then I was stuck. Ginny will leave me if she finds out." He suddenly remembered Emmett wondering how the clan had known where Trina was and knew that was it.

"Tell Ryker. He'll help." His tongue felt thick, and the words slurred. He realized he'd closed his eyes and forced them open. "Please," he whispered.

"Hush. Shut your eyes and relax." TJ released his grip but Darriel didn't have the strength to move. "You're just going to sleep for a bit."

Darriel's eyes were closing. "Why?" he mumbled.

"The clan and this shifter are my only hope. Zeke's getting him and I know that means Zeke will tell Ryker where they're meeting. Well, when I have you, he'll have no choice but to lie. You'll be taken care of. They promised."

Darriel was going to respond, laugh, argue, something, *anything*, but his last thought was that in trying to keep Zeke safe he was going to cause his death. He wasn't sorry when he felt himself sliding away from all that pain.

# Chapter Sixteen

After an hour Zeke got on the highway, double checked his mirror, and spoke to May confirming the funds were ready to be moved from the fictitious account as soon as he ordered it. Then he called Ryker at the pre-arranged point, knowing he would be waiting for the signal to shift. "Who was it?"

"We can't find anything," Ryker admitted. "If it's a panther shifter and all the claw are accounted for, I'm not surprised none of us can pick up a scent. I think Emmett was jumping at shadows."

"I think it was them and I think they left when I did," Zeke said dryly. "I noticed a silver truck about thirty minutes or so ago. Three behind me but it's still there."

"Could be anyone though."

"It could but when the guy behind me turned off, instead of closing the gap, the truck turned into a gas station. Barely a minute later he was back."

"Makes sense I guess," Ryker said. "They won't want you out of their sight."

Zeke tapped the steering wheel lightly. "Do you think they were checking on Trina?" *Or me?*

"If it is the Stanzas then they probably want to make sure you're leaving on your own."

"How long until you follow?"

"Sam and Fox have left in the bus and Chrissy's truck as we agreed because the brothers don't know them. Fox is your transport. Sam will meet you the second you clear the compound and take Bodhi to safety. TJ is waiting a little way off with the rescue truck in case any of the omegas are injured. Maybe twenty minutes behind you. I'll warn them about the silver truck. Regina's going to stay here because the worst thing is we don't know who's feeding them information, so she, Trina, and Emmett need to be visible to keep the claw here and protect the compound. "Red and I are shifting as soon as we finish talking. Chrissy and Mills River are making sure the pack area is secure."

"How's Darriel?" He imagined Ryker being surprised it hadn't been the first question out of his mouth. He didn't know how he'd managed it himself.

"He went for a rest before it all went down, as you know. The others are in the kitchen with all the kids. They know there's something up. Emmett is getting suspicious and he's trying to hide it in front of the others. I hate lying to him."

Zeke nodded. He hoped Darriel was getting some rest, or at least Emmy was letting him sleep.

"Maybe get Emmett to check on him?" He'd seemed upset. "Emmy doesn't let him sleep for long at a time."

"Oh no, it's okay. Emmett's got the girls with him."

Something cold slithered through Zeke. "Emmett's got Karina and Emmy," he clarified.

"Yes. I said they're all okay."

If Zeke hadn't been driving, he would have closed his eyes in horror. *"Because they're my responsibility and I ask them enough."*

He glanced in the rear-view mirror. The same silver truck was still three cars back. He couldn't risk stopping. "Ryker, go check on Darriel, *right now.*"

"Got it." The line went dead. Through the mirror, Zeke glanced at his empty back seat, then eyed the trunk. He wouldn't? It was *impossible*. There was no way Darriel would have done something so dangerous. They didn't know what Bodhi was for sure, and there hadn't been time for him to even get in there. It was far more likely he'd gotten in the back of Chrissy's truck. They kept tarpaulins, blankets, and basic medical and survival supplies in there. Easy enough for Darriel to hide in there... "Fuck," Zeke snapped out as he realized that was impossible. He couldn't hide from TJ and Fox because they could *smell* him.

But Zeke obviously couldn't. Then he remembered Emmett sighting the panther. Had that been a distraction? *But I'm being followed.*

Ryker called and didn't mess about. "He's gone, and I'm about to have a heart to heart with my *mate*." Ryker sounded furious.

"You can't," Zeke said. "Leave that to Chrissy. I need you and Red as back up. I'm altering the plan though. I'm not going to drive into the yard. I'll park it outside and walk in."

*"He's in the car?"* Ryker sounded appalled.

"I don't know, and I can't stop and find out. But he can't be with anyone else, can he? They'd smell him. Get Chrissy to find out what they know. I don't think we kept this as much a secret as we thought. Darriel must have known I was coming here, but I need you two to get him the fuck out of here."

"On it." Ryker said and rang off.

Zeke glanced in the mirror just in time to see the silver truck turn off, but did he dare risk it? He couldn't absolutely guarantee he wasn't being followed. He turned quickly at the last second into a gas station and ignored the horns honking at him in outrage. He pulled up at a pump and turned the engine off. He didn't move, just listened. "Darriel? I know you're in there."

Silence.

He watched the cars passing. No one had turned in after him, so he risked it and got out, looking for all the world like he was about to pump gas. In fact, that was a good idea and he quickly put ten dollars' worth in to look convincing. Then casually, he grabbed a jacket from the back seat and walked to the trunk as if putting it in there. He didn't breathe as he opened it, tossed the jacket in, and calmly got back in behind the wheel.

He pulled out and immediately called the pack house. Chrissy answered. "They know about Bodhi, and they had this crazy idea that you were going to try and rescue him on your own. Darriel was convinced Bodhi might be too terrified to leave with you."

Which he should have known. "Is Darriel there?"

"No, we've gone through the house."

*Fuck.* Where the hell was he?

"And Red and Ryker are running as wolves. I can't get them until they shift back."

"What vehicles have left? Any you weren't expecting? And are the other pack ones all accounted for?"

"TJ's driving the rescue truck and Fox has the bus so we have at least two big vehicles for the omegas so we can bring them back here. Sam is in mine to get Bodhi as soon as you have him. None of those three have been seen by the brothers in case plans change and you need any of them, but TJ's keeping the rescue vehicle out of the way because it's so recognizable. There's no other vehicle missing."

"If he's gone, he had to go in a vehicle because he can't shift."

"He can't hide in one either. All three of them would have gotten his scent immediately."

"Which means someone has him." Zeke said flatly. Chrissy didn't answer but she didn't have to. He looked at the time on the car. "I'll be there in forty minutes." Should he turn around?

"Zeke," Chrissy's voice was the gentlest he'd ever heard it. "There's nothing you could do if you came back. You do what you need, and I won't stop looking. We've got Mills River here."

He nodded then realized Chrissy couldn't see him. "I'll be in touch."

It was going to kill him. He'd thought he was okay to do this knowing Darriel was safe, but now? Zeke rang Chrissy back one more time before he approached the gates to the compound and there was no news. She'd gotten hold of TJ, Sam, and Fox and they were all close. She expected Ryker to check in with her as soon as he and Red were shifted back. Zeke pulled his car right up to the huge black gates and stared dispassionately at the scruffy looking tattooed guy walking up and down with a Rottweiler. He almost rolled his eyes. May had a huge Rotty she called Tiny. He was the softest ball of fur Zeke had ever met. He might lick you to death.

The gates, however, slid open and, taking his foot off the brake, Zeke let the car move forward. He stopped next to the pick-up he'd seen the brothers drive before and, taking a deep breath, got out. He reached back in for his briefcase and when he straightened up, he had a gun pointing right at him.

He arched an eyebrow at Paxton Davies, who was standing next to the skinny runt with the gun, and Paxton grinned. "We just need to check you're not bringing any nasty surprises. Paxton made a great show of patting him down and the other guy looked in the car, flipping the trunk. Of course, other than Zeke's jacket, it was empty. Zeke was guided inside, and he followed Paxton into an office? Study? Two huge leather wingback chairs sat opposite a huge flat screen TV and to the left there must have been six computer screens all jostling for position on an untidy desk. There were at least five different open beer cans acting like paperweights and three over-flowing ashtrays.

Zeke didn't react, simply turned and sat—reluctantly—in one of the chairs just as Porter appeared from the other door.

"Well?" he said rather unhelpfully and looked at his brother.

"I am here to negotiate," Zeke said, taking charge of the conversation immediately. "My client would like to know your starting number."

Porter picked up one of the empty beer-can paperweights and shook it to see if there was any left. "What's the name of this client?"

Zeke, who was just getting some papers out of his briefcase, looked up, sighed, stuffed his papers back in his vegan leather Entrussimo and stood. "I was clearly mistaken. I will see myself out."

Paxton responded completely predictably. "Hey buddy, it's all cool. We don't need to know." He shot a quelling look at his brother.

Zeke pretended to be hesitant until Porter muttered a little defensively. "Was just curious."

He nodded his acceptance of their apology and sat back down. "Starting number?"

"A million large," Porter said brashly and belched.

"If," Zeke said slowly, "my client was to consider that number, he would want additional assets."

Paxton looked blank but Porter huffed. "How many?"

"That would depend," Zeke said consideringly. "On what you have and their provenance." He made sure that by not so much as one flicker of an eyelash would his personal disgust betray him. "The younger the better. Virgins, obviously."

Paxton swallowed heavily and glanced at Porter. "We might have a couple."

"Out of how many?" Zeke responded, trying desperately not to look like he was swallowing nausea down...even though he was. He was a step away from putting his fist into each of their faces.

Paxton glanced at Porter. "Five of them."

Zeke nodded. "My client will take them all. What else do you have in your collection?" He was going to be physically sick. For a very long moment he debated asking where the bathroom was. "What other assets do you have available?" he repeated and looked at his watch, all the while trying to still his heart. Then he remembered they weren't shifters. It didn't matter. They couldn't hear his heartbeat.

"Well," Paxton said slowly. "We might be interested in getting out of this business. Our contact went and got himself killed and we're a bit short—ugh." He glared at Porter, who had just elbowed his brother in the ribs, but Zeke could guess at what the problem was. They'd lost their shifter contact—Riggs was dead—and all the conspiracy theory shit was just cover. They were in this for the money, which meant buying and *selling*. And they were stuck. In fact, it wouldn't surprise Zeke if the idiots were fishing for a replacement Riggs when they'd made up the story about the land. It made sense.

"We bought a parcel of land over near Kentucky. Lots of empty spaces for hiding certain things if you've a mind to do so."

Zeke could nearly have written the script. "Much as you may be dismayed, I have zero interest in any other business dealings at the moment other than the one we are currently negotiating. I would, however, be interested, depending on the successful conclusion of this one." He tried to sound bored, but he saw the gleeful look Paxton sent his brother. "My client is expecting me to call. How many and how much?" Was it really going to be this easy? He didn't even care about the money. Dollars were just bits of paper. His fortune was back at the pack house. Or he'd better be. *Darriel?* Where the hell are you?

Paxton shot another look at his brother. "If you're gonna clean us out it will cost you." Zeke waved a hand to mean of course. Paxton got up as quickly as his belly allowed. He nodded to his brother and they both left the room.

He would need Fox to come get them. At least neither of the Davies would know they were dealing with shifters. The problem was Bodhi's reaction, and he had a plan for that.

The brothers both lumbered back into the room. Or Paxton lumbered, Porter just slunk. "A million five and you can take 'em as soon as you want."

Zeke stared at Porter. It wasn't the first time he'd wished he was a shifter so he could more easily take out the trash. "Agreed. I have to arrange for transport, of course."

"None of those fuckers we met the other day," Paxton decreed.

"Hardly," Zeke scoffed. "This arrangement doesn't concern them." Porter smiled and left. Paxton eyed him curiously.

"So, how'd you find out about them, then? Kid says you're not one."

"I saw one of them shifting," Zeke lied. "I guess the same as you."

Paxton grunted. "I ain't seen none. Porter has though. He got in with someone who's let us down. They can't be trusted, you know."

"I don't trust anyone," Zeke said mildly and got his phone from his pocket. "I am arranging a pickup now. As soon as the goods are brought out, I will make the transfer."

"Tell 'em to pull in. We'll open the gates."

Fifteen minutes later Zeke stood by the entrance as Fox pulled in. A large group of males, some that looked the same age as Darriel, some that looked barely teenagers were marched out by the human guards. Bodhi was stumbling and one of the ones around his age was visibly holding him up. Fox jumped down from the bus without so much as looking in Zeke's direction and slid open the back door. Bodhi reacted predictably at Fox, giving Zeke the exact justification he needed to intervene.

"I want this one with me." Fox shot him a confused look because he didn't know the whole plan, but Zeke stepped up to Bodhi. *Close.* Now was the time to prove those renowned scenting abilities. He'd met Darriel and would remember his scent. The fact that Zeke would have Darriel's scent all over him should help. Then there was also the fact that he wasn't a shifter. He saw Bodhi's nostrils flare a little and stood perfectly still. Porter scowled.

"Get your lazy ass in that car or I put a bullet in Kit." One of the smaller boys gasped in fear loud enough to get Bodhi's attention. The look Bodhi shot the younger boy made Zeke want to put a bullet in Porter. It was full of simple acceptance, like he expected nothing better to happen to him. Porter opened Zeke's trunk and Bodhi got in without a word. Zeke opened his mouth to protest but then he closed it. As soon as he was clear he would pull up and get him out, make sure he was okay.

In the end, the leaving was simple. Fox crammed the boys in the bus and they both pulled out of the compound. Zeke let Fox pull ahead then slowed and looked for somewhere to safely pull up and meet Ryker and Sam as arranged.

Sam would get the boy away and Zeke would go to the meeting point, and the wolves would do the rest. He was just going to lure them in. TJ was in the rescue truck with all the medical equipment just in case any of the omegas needed it.

He knew Ryker and the others were shifted and waiting but they couldn't do anything until he had a location.

When his phone rang barely a second later it was almost a relief to get it over with. "Coleman."

"Zeke?" He frowned, struggling to place the voice for a moment.

"It's TJ." His heart jumped. Had they found Darriel? "Ryker just shifted to ask where I was. He's spoken to Fox, and he says you have the boy, but he didn't look too good when you picked him up. I have to meet you with the rescue truck and take him rather than wait for Sam. He's worried he might have a panic attack and hurt himself."

"I was just going to get him out," Zeke said. "They put him in the trunk."

He heard TJ swear. "I see you. If you carry on up ahead there's a small motel with a large empty parking lot around the back. Drive around the back of the dumpsters so you can't be seen. I'll meet you there, grab Bodhi, and then you can go."

"Is there any news on Darriel?" Zeke burst out.

"No, sorry, but I'm sure they'll find him." Zeke wanted to scream. He needed this done so he could find him himself. He snapped off the phone then swore in frustration as he saw it ring again as he pulled into the motel and around the back by the dumpsters.

"Coleman."

"Zeke, where are you? Is Bodhi okay?"

"Meeting TJ so he can get him," Zeke snapped out at Fox, wanting to be off the damn phone. He pulled behind the dumpsters as close as he could, watching TJ pull the truck right behind him to stay hidden. He saw TJ open the door and jump out.

"TJ?" Fox replied. "I thought it was going to be Sam?"

"Ryker called him and told him to meet me. He was worried about the state Bodhi was in." Zeke opened the door and opened his door.

"But that's not possible," Fox said. "Ryker's not here yet. They're still shifted. There's no way he would even know what state Bodhi was in. Zeke—" But Zeke couldn't answer because as he stepped out, he came face to face with the gun TJ was pointing a gun at him. TJ reached over and took the phone, clicking it off. He tossed it back to him, but Zeke made no move to catch it. It skittered toward Zeke's shoes.

"Call them."

Zeke folded his arms and made no attempt to pick up the phone.

TJ lifted the gun higher. "I said call them."

"No. I don't know what you've done, but they're crazy, murderous bastards I wouldn't give my worst enemy to." TJ took a step to the trunk and pointed the gun at it. The threat was clear.

"You put a bullet in him, and you've got nothing left for whoever's paying you." Zeke knew he was right even though his heart was hammering like a drum and for all he knew TJ could hear it. But TJ nodded as if in agreement.

"That's very true," he admitted, stepping back to the rescue truck and keeping the gun on Zeke. For an insane moment Zeke thought he was going to leave, but he opened the back door and with the strength of a shifter, dragged the unconscious young man out and held him up against his body like a shield.

Zeke's heart, which had been pounding against his ribs as if it wanted to escape, simply stopped. For an interminable second all Zeke could hear was white noise and he took an involuntary step forward. He jerked to a stop when TJ pressed the barrel against Darriel's temple.

"Call them."

Zeke stared at the phone and bent, reaching out, but before his fingers touched it, he heard another voice. The one from his nightmares.

"Oh, I don't think that will be necessary, Mr. Coleman." He looked up and the panther shifter who had tormented him stepped up, flanked by two others. He had no doubt they were claw.

The panther glanced at TJ and tilted his head assessingly. "And who's this?"

"It's his mate," TJ rushed out. "They've got an ambush planned. I knew if I could use him to threaten Zeke, he would give the omega up and we could get away."

The panther didn't answer, merely nodded to one of his men and they walked unconcerned to the trunk, opening it, and lifting Bodhi out. Bodhi's legs gave way and he gazed in horror, not at the claw, but at Darriel.

The panther stared at TJ and nodded to Darriel. "Let him go." TJ slackened his grip as if he was just going to let Darriel drop, and Zeke lunged for him at the same time as a shot rang out and TJ was flung back six feet. He caught Darriel and curled his body over him, trying to shield him from the flying bullets. He rocked forward as a sharp pain shoved him into Darriel, but he flung his arms out so he wouldn't crush him. Darriel blinked open his eyes, but Zeke didn't have the time to appreciate it.

The panther shifter leveled his gun at Zeke and smiled. "It was fun, but you got boring when you capitulated so fast. Put him in the car." the panther ordered, and Zeke looked to his left and saw one of the panthers dragging a struggling Bodhi away, and Zeke's brain whirled with the need to get Darriel to safety. "Take me," he demanded. "Just let him go. You can do whatever you like to me." Because it didn't matter. He would spend his life in chains so long as Darriel and their child were safe.

His tormentor smiled lazily. "Stand up." Zeke got to his feet and watched the gun lower to fire, then the panther's eyes widened in sudden shock as a huge red wolf followed by two even bigger panthers seemed to appear from absolutely nowhere.

One of the other panther's holding Bodhi fired his gun, only for it to be ripped from his hand, including the whole arm that was holding it, by huge teeth. Two claw leapt on top of the body and finished it off. In the middle of snarls and screeches, fur flying, blood spraying, Zeke bent and pulled Darriel close, and reached out to yank a cowering Bodhi to him, but he never got the chance because the huge red wolf that had killed the panther holding Bodhi suddenly shifted back into a human and gathered Bodhi into his arms.

Zeke lifted his head to gauge and see if he could reach the truck, just as the man who had tormented him aimed his gun right at Zeke's head. Zeke had a second to register a massive black wolf he recognized sail over their heads and hit the panther so hard they rolled. When they stopped the wolf spat out the ripped throat his teeth had clamped on and looked up.

Zeke lifted his head and stared at the carnage that had taken mere seconds and his knees wobbled. He fell to the side, feeling Darriel's arm on his but he couldn't seem to make his body stay upright.

Ryker immediately shifted, followed by Sam, and two panthers. One came to stand behind the smaller black panther who stood defiantly facing up to a very pissed off Ryker. He glared at the second huge panther partially shielding the smaller one from Ryker.

"Don't bother," he barked out in fury at the panther and turned to the smaller one. "Because Regina is going to fucking kill me when she finds out."

# Chapter Seventeen

D arriel shook himself and took in the scene. He could see the blood, the dead shifters. He looked to his side and saw TJ, but quickly looked away and swallowed the sickly moisture that filled his throat. He saw Red cradling Bodhi then realized he wasn't surprised. Bodhi was just lying there dazed, staring up at the big wolf who didn't look like he was going to put the omega down anytime soon.

He heard a small noise to his side and turned to smile at Zeke. He'd known instinctively who held him. They were both lying on the trash-strewn ground but it didn't seem important when they were both alive. Together. Darriel raised a hand to stroke Zeke's face. "You did it."

Zeke grimaced as he tried to move but brought his own hand to clutch Darriel's arm. "I nearly lost you. What," he paused and panted out a breath "would I have done?"

"Are you two planning on getting up off the ground or are you taking a nap?" Ryker drawled and held his hand out to Darriel. Darriel smiled and let himself be pulled up. Ryker swore. "What the

164

hell? Where are you hurt?" Darriel looked down at his shirt that was mattered with a big crimson stain and paled.

"Get it off," Ryker pulled but Darriel pushed his hands away as complete panic slammed into him.

"It isn't me," and they both seemed to realize Zeke was still on the ground. He hadn't gotten to his feet when Ryker had pulled Darriel off him, and he didn't look like he could. Darriel dropped to his knees and took Zeke's cold and clammy hand in his. "Zeke," he whispered but was pushed to the side as Sam and Ryker took over. One of the claw ran to the rescue truck and hoisted the huge box of equipment over as if it was nothing.

Ryker swore but came around to Darriel and they both tilted Zeke over to them so Sam could see his back. Darriel concentrated on Zeke's face and bent down kissing him gently. "I love you."

Zeke smiled, but his skin was paper white, and his breaths were labored and barely there. His eyes started closing as Darriel held him. "Zeke," Darriel yelled. "You look at me." He needed Zeke's eyes on him, but they slid closed once more and Darriel grabbed his shoulder in desperation. "Damn it, open your eyes." He let out a sob that seemed to tear him in half and looked up just to see Sam look helplessly at Ryker.

"The bullet's gone right through but I think it's nicked his lung and maybe his artery. He's human."

"He's my mate," Darriel almost screamed and shook Zeke's shoulder. "Don't you die. Don't you *fucking* die."

People were opening pads and pressing them to open wounds. Trina even called 911 because it was Zeke and none of their shifter abilities could help. Darriel refused to let go of him, willing him to live. He couldn't leave him.

"You're going to be a daddy," Darriel whispered. "I can't do it on my own."

Then everyone fell silent and Darriel looked up as Bodhi bent down over Zeke's still form. Red was hovering but Bodhi looked a little stronger. He met Darriel's eyes. "He's your mate?"

Darriel nodded through his tears.

"Then give him your blood."

For a second no one responded. "But he's human," Ryker said in bewilderment. "How—"

Bodhi ignored him and took Darriel's wrist. "I can hear his heartbeat. *Both* their heartbeats." It took Darriel a very long second to work out he meant the baby then nodded and thrust his wrist at Sam.

"Cut me." Sam looked in utter confusion at Ryker. "Do it," Darriel yelled but Ryker didn't wait, lifting Darriel's arm and with one claw that pushed from his first finger, he sliced Darriel's arm. Blood gushed immediately and Darriel pressed it to Zeke's lips. It went everywhere. It dripped down Zeke's chin and slid down his neck. Darriel looked helplessly at Ryker. Zeke wasn't swallowing.

"Zeke, damn you," Ryker swore and pressed a hand over Zeke's throat, but nothing happened, so Bodhi simply pressed his hand over Zeke's heart. Zeke jerked, swallowed, and coughed, then took some more. They all looked up as sirens were heard but no one moved. Bodhi lay another shaking hand on Zeke's chest then nodded.

"Stop," he whispered. Get him home." Darriel slumped to the side, only half aware of Sam picking him up and putting him on one of the seats. Zeke was fastened onto the stretcher and Ryker jumped in beside him, taking Darriel's arm and pressing a pad to it to stop the bleeding. Sam followed them inside and started pulling out equipment. Doors slammed and engines roared. Ryker put his arm around Darriel's shoulders to keep him safe while someone drove the truck like a madman. Darriel pulled away from Ryker and knelt on the floor next to the stretcher. Sam didn't seem to object as he set up IV's and bags of blood and the heart monitor.

And all the while Darriel just held Zeke's hand and refused to let it go as they drove up the mountain. He didn't let go when Marco met them and they took Zeke into the clinic, and when Emmett came and sat beside him. He looked up then, expecting Emmett to want to take his dad's hand. To claim him. To tell Darriel he had no right, but Emmett just put his arm around Darriel and whispered his thanks.

And that was what started the tears. But even as Emmett held him tight and rocked him, he still held onto Zeke's fingers. He wasn't ever letting go again.

He felt like he'd come in a complete circle, Zeke mused, opening his eyes and seeing his surroundings. Except this was an improvement. Being pillowed on Darriel's shoulder was so much better than staring at the blank clinic walls. He blinked and focused. In fact...he wasn't in the clinic. He was in his bed at the pack house. When had that happened?

He listened for the sound of sleeping babies and smiled when he heard a faint snuffle from one of the cribs. Still dark outside so early. He remembered everything from last night, or at least he remembered up to the point of hearing Ryker swearing at Trina. He didn't know how she'd gotten there, but he'd be dead if she hadn't. The wolves wouldn't have gotten there in time. Something had happened to his back—again—but he wasn't in any pain. In fact, he'd never felt better. Must be the way he'd woken up and he wondered how long it would be until Darriel did. He slid a hand gently over his belly. Was he imagining the slight roundness? Probably. He knew omega pregnancy was faster with more concentrated symptoms but if they had gotten pregnant the first time it hadn't even been three weeks, and that was a generous estimation.

He carried on with his light perusal of Darriel's warm, soft skin until his fingers headed lower and he smiled at what he touched. Darriel was hard, and he rocked against him.

Darriel opened his eyes and reached over meeting his lips. "How are you feeling?"

Zeke rocked against him once more, letting a certain part of his anatomy answer his mate's question. Darriel smirked and slid his own hand in between them. "What do you remember?"

"Trina being a bad ass. Ryker losing his shit." He frowned. "It was a little hazy after that. Did something happen to me?"

167

"You were shot protecting me," Darriel whispered, and his eyes glittered with sudden moisture.

Zeke searched his brain but came up blank, then he wriggled his shoulders a little. "Then I must be on some good drugs because I don't feel like I took a bullet."

"It's complicated," Darriel hedged but he looked so cute and tasted so good that Zeke didn't care and in one move rolled over straddling him, their cocks brushing together because they were happily naked. Zeke smiled his approval and bent, pressing their erections together and kissing his gorgeous mate but anchoring his arms at either side of Darriel so he didn't give him his full weight. Not on Darriel's belly anyway.

They explored each other's mouths and rubbed their cocks together, slick quickly forming and easing Zeke's movements. He sat back and pushed Darriel's knees up and apart, then dipped his head and explored Darriel's body until Darriel was biting his lip not to cry out. Zeke shook a little not with exhaustion or nerves, but with a nearly overwhelmingly intense need to be inside Darriel. "Yes," Darriel gasped as if Zeke had asked him, and he needed no further urging, lining up and sliding home. He stilled, Darriel's hot, utterly perfect channel gripping him tight until Darriel moved restlessly, his small moans more intoxicating than the brandy he occasionally indulged in. Zeke slid back a little then pushed in harder. Darriel whined, trying to stifle his cries, so Zeke bent down and continued to thrust, swallowing all of Darriel's cries, his whimpers, and then his pleasure.

Zeke gasped as his own orgasm clutched his insides and forced heat and light and pure bliss through every nerve, every cell, and seemed to settle in his heart. He collapsed to the side of Darriel, but taking him with him, wrapping him up and promising he would never ever let him go.

. . .

A small, indignant noise made Zeke aware a few moments later and he cracked open an eyelid at the two feet stuck up in the air and trying to fight to get free of the blanket. He chuckled, happy beyond everything that he was getting to experience something other dads did the world over. Not that their new house wouldn't have a separate nursery, he allowed. Because he had every intention of waking up like this for as many mornings as were physically possible. He sat up as Darriel opened his eyes, hearing the same thing. "I'll get them."

An hour later, after breakfast Zeke, Ryker, Chrissy, Fox, and Regina were sitting finishing their coffees in the office. Marco, Darriel, and Red were with Bodhi, who was still mostly terrified of everyone except Darriel and Red.

Zeke had been rendered temporarily speechless—a feat worth remarking on—as Ryker had explained exactly what had happened last night and the possible explanations.

"You're saying," Zeke said slowly "That the reason I'm not only alive but have nearly a completely healed back in the space of twelve hours is because I drank blood?" He gazed at Regina. "I thought you guys were shifters not freaking vampires."

He wasn't surprised when no one laughed. It hadn't been a joke.

"Not just blood, your *mate's* blood," Chrissy pointed out.

"Even so," Zeke said. "I know about the mating bite, but this is a little far-fetched. And," he waved a hand at himself. "Human?"

"I suppose that's a matter of opinion," Regina drawled. "Given the fact that your wolf shifter omega is expecting a baby. And I have no doubt the healing wouldn't have worked at all without the presence of the Khan-re."

"Except he isn't yet, is he?" Fox interrupted. "Didn't you say because he can't shift, he hasn't imprinted or whatever."

Regina nodded. "The problem is that this is so wrapped up in legend and myth I honestly don't know what's true and what isn't. Shifters of the same species generally mix blood during the mating bite, but they don't necessarily drink it, and I have never seen or heard of such a ritual or such an astonishing result before." She hesitated. "But the legends associated with the Khan included incredible abilities."

Zeke must have made some disbelieving noise because Ryker glanced at him. "I don't know what you remember from last night buddy, but you were basically screwed. The bullet had nicked not just an artery, but Sam thought your lung as well. Whatever Bodhi and Darriel did between them it saved your life. We'd even called 911 but the ambulance wouldn't have gotten there in time. You'd stopped breathing."

Zeke ran a hand through his hair in bewilderment. It was incredible, certainly, and he felt good, very good. He remembered Marco's surprise after he had examined him that morning. Marco had told him by the time Ryker had carried him to his room the wound had been healing already.

"What are we going to do about Bodhi?" Chrissy asked.

"I made some confidential inquiries last night," Regina said. "I'm waiting for a call from my contact."

"He seems to be close to Red."

Ryker smiled but Regina leaned forward. "Ryker, you have to warn Matthew not to get too involved."

"Matthew?"

Ryker glanced at Zeke. "Red. Regina refuses to use nicknames."

"I think it might be a little late," Fox said.

Regina whipped her head around. "I hope that was a joke."

Fox lifted his hands in a surrender motion. "I didn't mean like that. Red wouldn't lay a finger on him, least of all a mating bite. I meant he was on guard duty all night." Fox looked at Ryker pleadingly.

Ryker sighed. "He hasn't said but I'm pretty sure they're mates, judging from Red's reaction."

"It won't be allowed," Regina said a little more calmly. "To become Khan, he has to mate a tiger. It's not possible any other way."

"What if he doesn't want to be this khan?" Zeke asked.

Regina didn't answer for a few moments but then she sighed. "You have to understand he cannot stay here. Until he becomes Khan-re at the very least he will be in great danger from every shifter group the world over. It's not possible to keep this quiet forever."

"Could you—" Zeke started but Regina was already shaking her head.

"This isn't another Trina situation. The thought of anyone getting their hands on him fills me with horror. We would be talking a war. Keeping our secrets from humans would be the least of our problems. We would be too busy trying to keep them alive."

Zeke leaned back in his chair. He honestly hadn't realized how serious this was.

"I also reached out to Jered. He's taking one of Ginny's friends this morning and going to break the news. She's going to be invited to Mills River if she wants. She won't be told what happened, just that he got caught in a rescue that went wrong."

"You think it was him who told the claw last year where Trina was?" Zeke asked.

"Yes. Jered has a place for her dad as well, and he'll be looked after," Ryker said. "He's sending some enforcers around to the loan shark. They won't be any trouble again."

Zeke wished he'd known TJ better and that he could have come to him for help, but he supposed because TJ had only recently joined Ryker's pack their paths hadn't crossed.

The knock on the door interrupted them all and Dinah put her head around. "Sorry, but the guys have called from the pack boundary. A black hummer just drove past and is heading this way."

Zeke met Ryker's gaze. Ryker turned to Fox. "I want the kids out of sight, and the omegas warned." He looked at everyone. "Let's go see who it is."

Zeke, stood with Ryker on the steps as the hummer drove up. He could see menacing-looking panther claw at the edge of the trees ready to intercept. He knew Chrissy and Fox had shifted. Everyone else was out of sight and guarded. Red had been warned and Darriel was with them.

Trina, however, joined Regina just behind them, completely refusing to hide. Loren, Asheel, Tam, and Hansa were on either side. It was an impressive, if formidable, welcoming committee. Zeke knew they'd all look stupid if it was someone inquiring about a land purchase, or hunting rights, which they occasionally still got. Ryker refused to put visible guards anywhere because it gave curious humans the idea that they had something to hide, and their biggest threat would be on four paws not two legs.

The hummer's windows were black, and Zeke held himself still as the driver got out, scanned the area including them, then turned and went around to the passenger door, opening it respectfully. He heard the sharp inhale from Regina as a man got out, more surprising because that was so un-Regina like to make any visible reaction, but as Zeke took him in, he wasn't surprised. The sheer power rolling off this man was palpable. Around the same height as Zeke, the black-haired giant's gaze flicked over everyone before he turned back and offered his hand.

The woman that took it and climbed out after him was simply stunning. Her long, wavy auburn hair flowed down her back, and her wide smile seemed to encompass everyone. She was as light-skinned as her mate was dark. He felt like he should bow or something, but as soon as she pinned her huge green-eyed gaze on him he knew exactly who she was. The same hued gaze—shadowed, terrified, but nearly identical—had glanced at him from the Davies brothers' compound. This, then, was the Khan and Bodhi's parents.

Ryker walked down the steps and extended his hand respectfully. The Khan took it but slid his hand up Ryker's arm and clasped it in a gesture Zeke had only ever seen a few times and only between alphas. "Alpha," the Khan murmured. Zeke turned to Bodhi's mother to find her watching him closely. Not sure what he'd done to warrant this attention he held out his hand. She barely grazed his fingers before turning excitedly to her mate.

"It's true."

The Khan dropped Ryker's arm and strode over to Zeke so fast it took a great deal of effort for him not to step back. Zeke met his gaze openly. "Where is my son?"

"If you'd like to come inside?" Ryker said.

The Khan stepped right up to Zeke threateningly and repeated the question, enunciating very clearly. "Where is my son?" Zeke didn't reply. He didn't respond to intimidation tactics.

"Khan," Regina said quietly. "He is safe. Inside. I'm sure you don't want to conduct this meeting out here."

The Khan's mate sent him such an imploring gaze, Zeke's resentment disappeared as he remembered quite clearly last year that he had been in their shoes, except he hadn't spent twenty years thinking he had lost a child as well as Josie. He couldn't imagine.

They stepped inside and then any questions were irrelevant because the door to the omega side opened and Red, Darriel, and Bodhi appeared. Red looked like he would kill anyone who got near them, and Darriel drew closer to Bodhi almost protectively. Bodhi's mom covered her mouth with her hand. She let out a strangled sob. Darriel let go of Bodhi and they both stumbled toward each other. Bodhi hissed in pain as they made contact, but he didn't step back, just closed his eyes and seemed to breathe her in as he stood in her embrace. Then cautiously, he lifted his own arms to encircle her and then hugged her just as tight as if he was compelled to do so. Zeke glanced at Ryker, wondering if they should give them some privacy, but a warm hand slid into his and he turned and kissed Darriel before Darriel could say a word.

"Son?"

Bodhi lifted his gaze and stared at the Khan. "I don't know," he said helplessly. "I don't even know who you are. I just felt the need to come out here and Matthew and Darriel helped me."

The Khan's eyes immediately found Red's and he clearly didn't like whatever he saw in them. "Perhaps we can sit down" Zeke said smoothly. "The meeting room is private and more comfortable." He walked confidently to it, not letting go of Darriel's hand. They all took seats. Bodhi sat between his mom and Darriel. Red just stood with his back to the wall behind them. The Khan sat next to his mate.

He took in everyone in the room, then addressed Ryker. "You have my gratitude. An old acquaintance of ours contacted us last night through your shifter council and we flew straight here." He gazed at Bodhi. "We do not live in the States, but we were visiting some years ago on a diplomatic mission with your shifter council when my wife Aadhya went into early labor. Our hosts were kind, but separated from all the khan, we couldn't perform the immediate imprint. Then we were betrayed by someone we trusted, and you were taken. The shifter that took you was later found dead and that was where our trail ran cold. We have visited this country every year in the hopes that we would be able to find you, or that we would someday be contacted by the kidnapper even."

Zeke and Ryker explained their dealings with the Davies brothers, that whatever else had happened it was clear that the brothers and even Riggs were unaware who or what Bodhi was.

"Perhaps we can offer you some refreshments?" Regina asked.

The Khan shook his head. "My apologies, but the helicopter is already on its way and will be here momentarily. My son needs medical attention and the bonding of all his khan. It has to be done very quickly because by the time he reaches twenty-seven it will be too late." Zeke's surprise must have shown on his face because Aadhya laughed and sent a loving glance to her son. "You are twenty-six in two months."

The Khan gazed at his son. "Male tigers don't thrive without the khan. This accounts for your smaller stature, but that is all temporary." He stood just as the sound of an engine could be heard.

"I'm leaving?" Bodhi whispered and shot a desperate glance at Red. Zeke's gut clenched in sympathy then mild annoyance as the Khan deliberately came to stand in front of his son, blocking Red's view of him and vice versa. Zeke understood he really did, but then

Bodhi surprised them all by ducking around him and walking right up to Red. "Thank you, Matthew." He held out a hand.

Red jerked out a nod and clenched his fingers seemingly in an effort not to touch him until Bodhi let his drop.

"Ma'am?" Zeke started in an effort to break the rising tension, but also because he was curious. "If I may ask, when we met you seemed to take that as an indication your son was here. I know a shifter's sense of smell is phenomenal but—"

She let out a peal of laughter and sent Darriel a smile. "Bodhi—"

"Aadhya."

She sent her mate a quelling look at his interruption. "These shifters saved our son's *life*, Rishi. It is the least we can do." She turned to Zeke as the noise from the helicopter got louder. "You accepted a life force last night."

Zeke frowned.

A shifter saved your life by giving you a part of themselves." Zeke turned to gaze at Darriel.

"They did," he agreed quietly.

"Sometimes that act is impossible without help," Aadhya said somewhat vaguely. "Bodhi must have been there to lend that help." She shrugged and gazed lovingly at her son, taking his hand and drawing him close. "Unbonded and yet your gifts are amazing already."

Bodhi looked doubtful and overwhelmed and Zeke didn't blame him. He looked back at Red, who was watching him with hungry eyes. Rishi moved to block Bodhi's view again and Aadhya led Bodhi out. They went to the door and Zeke gazed at the three Boeing AH-64 Apaches from which men who were definitely not human security spilled out.

As he knew how much those particular machines cost, he hazarded a guess his own wealth paled into insignificance compared to the Khan. They got on board barely seeming to give Bodhi any choice, he stopped watching, turning to pull Darriel into his arms. He had everything he needed right here, and no one could put a price on that.

He wouldn't mind taking Darriel on a helicopter ride, though.

As the choppers lifted, they all heard a noise behind them. Not exactly a growl, but guttural and full of pain. Red gazed at Ryker and there seemed to be some unheard communication pass between them. "No," Ryker exclaimed and took a step as if he was going to stop him. Red bowed his head and shifted on the spot. Ryker moved closer, but the huge wolf snarled at his alpha, turned, and disappeared into the trees. Ryker made no move to follow him.

"Do you want me to—" Fox started undoing his shirt, but Ryker shook his head.

"What did he say?" Zeke said. He knew it couldn't be translated into words, but Ryker often understood.

Ryker met Zeke's gaze with a despairing one. "He just said goodbye."

# Epilogue

Nearly four months later.

"I have something to show you." Zeke rolled over in bed and smirked.

Darriel snickered. "You showed me it plenty last night, or not exactly," he amended. He could feel Zeke's gorgeous cock but seeing it over his huge belly was impossible.

Zeke chuckled and kissed him. "You have a one-track mind."

"That's because I'm worried."

Zeke's eyebrows shot up. "About the birth."

"No," Darriel almost screeched. "Because I'm a blob. It's like a *blob* invasion in here. I haven't seen my feet for weeks." He knew he was whining but he was supposed to be "blooming." He'd spent every second of his last pregnancies in fear and this one was supposed to be different, but no, because he'd obviously been evil in a previous life he was *plagued*.

He'd even nagged Marco to prove to him he wasn't expecting quadruplets or something because he was the size of a whale. His ankles were swollen, his back was killing him as usual, his blood pressure kept giving Marco another reason to insist on bed rest, he'd had awful indigestion for the whole of month three, and he'd gotten *zits*. Well, they were gone now but Darriel knew his skin was something Zeke remarked upon, and it had been the last straw. The meltdown hadn't been pretty. Much like his face.

Okay so that was a teeny exaggeration, but the fact he got any made him feel thirteen and on top of now sleeping with a god... He looked at Zeke, who was watching him in bemusement, but whatever had happened that night between the dumpsters and the trash, and whatever secret sauce his blood or Bodhi or both had given Zeke, he looked and acted ten years younger. He was vital, strong, fun.

In fact, pretty much everything Darriel wasn't.

"Are you going to come and see?"

My back hurts," Darriel said sulkily.

"I can carry you," Zeke countered and Darriel sighed because he knew Zeke could. In fact, it seemed to be one of Zeke's favorite occupations. Next to sex. And kissing. He was pretty good at rubbing Darriel's feet as well. It wasn't fair that Zeke got to be so talented and Darriel had turned into a blob.

Darriel held his hand out and Zeke eased him up gently so he was sitting on the end of the bed and carefully put thick socks on him. Zeke looked up. "It's cold outside."

It was freezing. March wasn't being kind and they had even had fresh snow last week. The pups had loved it and the sight of a large black wolf chasing them while they all pelted Ryker with snowballs had been entertaining, or it had been, sitting in a comfy chair with his feet up and drinking hot chocolate while the girls sat in their bouncy chairs. He wasn't sure about actually going out in it.

Zeke had just returned from taking both of the girls to Charles since Mo still liked to hold Karina while Dr. Darling visited. Mo still hadn't spoken but the doc thought it would just take patience. The doc kept asking if Regina was free for a coffee or dinner. She hadn't accepted so far but he kept trying.

He struggled into his warmest sweats even with Zeke helping

him because his back ached worse than ever, then a shirt and a sweater, and finally a large thermal-lined coat that made him look nearly as round as he was tall. Omegas were supposed to be slim and alluring and—

"How's my heart?"

Darriel smiled despite himself. It was a thing between them. Zeke never asked if Darriel loved him, but proclaimed Darriel held his heart in his hands. Then he kissed his fingers, his palms and covered them with his own larger ones. "Safe as always," Darriel whispered and got a kiss as a reward for giving Zeke the right answer. Not that it was ever a difficult question.

Darriel headed for the bathroom to pee again because apparently his bladder was the size of an acorn, brushed his teeth, and stared at himself. He did look better. No dark shadows because a certain alpha made sure he was spoiled, well-rested, and very much loved. He noticed Zeke standing in the doorway watching him. He quirked an eyebrow.

"Just admiring my mate."

Darriel took a pleased breath. "What have you got to show me?" Zeke made him sit again to put his thermal boots on then stood, held out an arm, and Darriel took it. They left their room and walked through the kitchen, but instead of heading to the door, Zeke took him to the back.

"Where are we going?" He pressed his lips together to stop a grin. They'd been extending the property at the back and Zeke had casually asked Darriel what he'd thought about having their own apartment in the new build? Darriel had nodded eagerly but had been a tiny little bit disappointed because he had liked the idea of their own cabin and a little yard where Emmett or Kai could bring their kids to play. But Zeke could have whatever he wanted so long as Darriel was with him. He knew the units were finished. Ryker was going to let whoever wanted to look around today, but he wasn't surprised that Zeke wanted to show him first.

"It's better if we go this way," Zeke said when Darriel headed for the main path that took them to the front door. All of these apartments were large family suites for long-term use. If the omegas and their families wanted to settle in a cabin they could do so, including the ones being built on the new area of land complete with the new school and secondary clinic area.

Darriel followed Zeke around the path to the side that normally led straight into the forest until Zeke stopped just before they turned a corner. He turned to face him. "Close your eyes." Zeke took both of Darriel's hands and guided him forward. Darriel stepped forward with no hesitation. Zeke wouldn't let anything happen to either of them.

"Okay." Darriel opened his eyes and Zeke stood to the side. Darriel stared awestruck at the building in front of him. It was a cabin, but not a tiny one like Ryker's old one, and even bigger than the one Emmett and Ryker had at the front. He took in the way it faced away from the new build for privacy. The yard, complete with brand new swing sets, the snowdrops that lined the front path, and the huge windows of the top floor. Darriel pressed a hand to his mouth because this wasn't a day for crying, even though they would be happy tears.

"Come see." Zeke sounded so excited and Darriel let him lead him into the large family kitchen with plenty of room for family dinners. He examined the mud room just off it that had a smaller door to the yard, the sleek office for Zeke, the cozy den with the large fireplace, and the family room complete with huge TV and squishy sofas.

Then he led him to the stairs. "Do you need help?"

Darriel shook his head, back-ache forgotten in the wonder of what he was seeing, and nearly danced up the staircase holding tightly to Zeke's hand. There were five bedrooms. Three smaller ones that all led off a large playroom, a separate guest suite, then theirs. Darriel gaped when he went in and walked right up to the huge floor to ceiling windows that looked out over the trees and the mountain beyond.

"It's privacy glass so you don't need to worry about anyone seeing you dancing naked." He gathered Darriel in his arms and gently swayed from side to side. "What do you think?"

Darriel looked up and smiled, wondering which information to share first. "Two things. Firstly, It's the most beautiful house I've ever seen, and you're incredibly sneaky." Zeke had asked him casually about carpets and paint colors and all sorts of things over the last few months. He'd thought it was for the apartment though. "I am the luckiest man in the world." Zeke shook his head.

"Nope, that'd be me." Darriel took a deep breath and hid his wince from Zeke. "Was that the second thing," Zeke murmured kissing Darriel's head.

"No," Darriel said a little breathlessly. "The second thing is we're going to have a baby."

Zeke chuckled. "Yeah, I got that." He tipped Darriel's chin slightly and pressed their lips together, still swaying gently to imagined music. "I've known that for a few months."

Darriel nodded and took another steadying breath. "No, what I mean is we're going to have a baby like really soon."

"Ten days according to Marco." Zeke sighed happily.

"Uh-huh, well he's nine days off."

It took Zeke a moment then he pushed Darriel to arm's length. "*What?*" He raked his gorgeous blue-gray eyes up and down Darriel. "You—"

Darriel nodded. "So unless you want me to spoil our new carpet I suggest you get me back to our rooms." Zeke bent but Darriel stopped him. "I can walk."

"I know but why would you," Zeke said and swung Darriel up into his arms and then grinned. "You gave me your strength now it's my turn to give you mine. Do you want me to call Emmett?" Darriel shook his head as Zeke carefully navigated the stairs, house, the path and got them back into their room.

"No, Emmett and I talked and he and Kai are going to watch the kids so Charles can be here, as well as you, obviously."

Zeke sat Darriel on the bed and started unwrapping him. "That's a good thing to do."

Darriel smiled, then his first proper pain hit, and everything paused while Zeke helped him through it. As soon as he was comfy with a discreet pad laid under him because his water hadn't broken yet, Zeke made the phone calls as asked. Charles, Marco, and Ryker all turned up in moments. Ryker said he'd leave them to it, but he was here if they needed him. Marco just kept casually checking on him but didn't hover. Charles was so touched to be asked and took care of Darriel's comfort and the practicalities. Zeke breathed with him through every pain, held his hand, rubbed his back, and then as Marco instructed, got in bed behind Darriel first to prop him up and then so he could turn over onto all fours and hang onto Zeke.

Caden Wilder (after Zeke's grandad) Coleman was born five hours later to ecstatic parents and a stunned Marco because Caden weighed nine pounds four ounces. Completely unheard of from a male omega birth, with a huge, noisy set of lungs to match. Darriel finally let himself cry the tears of happiness he's been holding back when Marco showed him how to position Caden to his swollen nipple and he started sucking. The room fell silent as everyone stood and watched in awe.

Marco finished what he needed to do, and Charles left with him to give the proud parents some privacy before they started letting visitors in. It was perfect.

"How's my heart?" Zeke whispered, sitting on the bed cradling Caden while Darriel dozed beside him.

"Full of love," Darriel murmured. "But you can't have it back. It's mine for keeps."

Two days later, Darriel was ensconced in the huge, comfy chair quietly feeding Caden surrounded by Emmett, Kai, and Charles with all the babies in their strollers. The room was a little full.

"It's a good thing you've got a house," Kai teased. "We're not all going to fit in here much longer."

"No," Emmett said with a knowing smile. "Not if we keep adding babies."

They all shot him surprised looks and Kai squealed, startling Maddox. "Really?"

Emmett blushed. "Yes."

That was followed by a round of hugs and congrats until Marco, Ryker, and Zeke stepped back into the room, and then more congratulations followed. Ryker looked very smug, but Darriel had seen that look on his own alpha a few times, so he wasn't surprised. Ryker took Emmett and Josie. Marco collected his troop and Zeke—now that Caden had finished—held him so Darriel could go pee and tidy up. When Darriel came back in he looked over at Zeke to see him studying him as if he were weighing up a decision. It made him pause. Zeke was one of the most confident people he knew. "What's wrong? Is it Red?" Red had never come back after he had run when Bodhi left with his parents. He knew Ryker went to search every so often, but he could be anywhere.

Shortly after Red had left, the Davies brothers had been found dead of a suspected wild animal attack. They'd both had their throats ripped out before they'd even had a chance to get a shot off. Darriel wasn't sorry. He just wished Red would come home. If Red's wolf really had chosen Bodhi as his mate even though they hadn't bonded, he could quite easily go feral without him.

Zeke laid Caden in his crib while Darriel sat back down. "Someone's here to see you."

"To see me?" Darriel said in surprise. "But I don't know anyone."

Zeke nodded. "You know lots of people, but this one took some finding." Darriel stared at Zeke. He looked nervous.

"Who?"

They both turned at the knock on the door and Ryker stepped in, holding the door open for the woman who followed him. Darriel gazed at her in utter disbelief. Zeke stood and held his hand out, guiding her to the chair next to Darriel. She sat and they just stared at each other. He swallowed. It wasn't possible. He glanced at Zeke, who was smiling, and nodded at him, so he turned back to the woman who was biting her lip and looking like she would cry.

*"Mom?"*

She choked out a word that might have been yes but got to her feet at the same time as Darriel got to his. "Mom," he repeated more confidently, and they both met in a tangle of arms and kisses and tears.

"Darriel, Darriel," she whispered over and over. "My baby."

"How about if we sit down?" Zeke said gently after a few minutes.

Darriel nodded then turned to Zeke. *"How?"*

"With the help of Morgan from Mills River."

"The alpha told me you were dead," she choked out, refusing to let go of his hand.

"That's what Riggs told me," Darriel confirmed. "After—" He looked at Zeke and Zeke nodded encouragement. "After Alpha Jered won the challenge last year, it was the first thing I asked when I was able. You definitely weren't there and the only thing they could find out was that one of the she-wolves had died and they said it was you."

She shook her head. "Riggs told me you'd tried to run and the gammas had killed you to make an example of you." Tears rolled down her cheeks. "When they took you, I was told never to mention you and given another name. If I said anything you would be punished."

"It was all lies," Zeke said. "Lies so no one could find out what Riggs was up to. His alpha wasn't any better, but Riggs was selling omegas under his nose. Only by not having records and such a high turnover could he hide it."

"One of the other she-wolves wanted to leave. She said she had no intention of staying a slave for the rest of her life, and we planned things together. I went to where we'd arranged to meet but the gammas had found her first." His mom shook her head. "The smell of the blood masked my scent, and I just ran. I eventually got taken in by a pack in Virginia, and when the Alpha-mate heard my story, she said she would do her best to help."

"With the help of what Morgan and Jered could tell me I put out feelers a couple of months ago. I didn't want to say anything because it could well have been true, but there's a mate of one of the betas there and she remembers a young woman getting beaten to death. Everyone said it was you, but she was friends with the she-wolf that wanted to leave and didn't believe it when they said she had mated and left the pack. Which Jered insisted was wrong because his uncle would never let anyone leave."

"Serena has permission from both her current alpha and from Ryker to stay here if she chooses."

Darriel didn't think his day could get any better. Serena wiped her eyes and smiled. "Now," she said taking a longing look at the crib. "Don't I have three gorgeous grandchildren to meet?"

When things had calmed down and all three babies were enjoying an afternoon nap, Darriel got into bed at Zeke's urging and snuggled up against him. "I can't believe you did that for me."

Zeke brushed a kiss over his lips. "I'd do anything for you."

"You know she's already offered to babysit?" Darriel said.

Zeke smirked. "That was my evil plan really. I needed to ensure we had some alone time." He lifted himself up on one elbow and traced a finger down Darriel's cheek.

"Why do we need alone time?" Darriel teased and he caught sight of a smile before Zeke bent down to fasten their lips together and show him *exactly* why.

Darriel—utterly content with such sound reasoning—wrapped his arms around him and showed his gorgeous human alpha exactly how much he agreed.

**Ready to see what happens with Red and Bodhi?** Click HERE to pre-order Baby and the Warrior! Available April 29th.

*Epilogue*

Don't miss out on the free prequel, **Baby and the Bear**:

Available as a free download at Bookfunnel or Prolific Works

# Excerpt from Hunter's Creek

## One

Asher grinned at his mom as he strode through the playroom to grab his mail. Half-buried in clothes of every size, she quickly sorted them into piles. Although, to be fair, they'd had kids of just about every size come through the doors of Hunter's Creek in the last fourteen years and that was while they were still human.

Familiar pride tugged at him. There were group foster homes the world over, but Hunter's Creek was a little different. Not that the rest of the world knew that though. He imagined Harriet Harker from the Montana Child and Family Services division wouldn't be the fan of this place she seemed to be if she knew the truth. Asher rolled his eyes at the understatement.

His mom smiled back as she disappeared with an armful of laundry. The phone rang in the office and he swiped it up, wondering where his brothers were. It was unusually quiet around the house. "Yeah?"

A laugh came down the line—*Brett.* "Only you, Asher, only you.

Your mom could never get you to answer the phone properly." Asher grinned, remembering all the times his mom had scolded him for not saying *Hunter's Creek* like some fancy secretary. "So how's it going? Thought you were on vacation." He chuckled, the small sound in the back of his throat directly from his animal for those that recognized it. The people who didn't thought he was possibly clearing his throat. Or laughing. There had been a few disgusted teachers when he was younger who thought he was making fun of them when nothing could have been further from the truth.

Brett chuckled. "I am, but I got a call, and I wondered if you could handle it? I can't get back for at least two days." Asher sat down and pulled a notepad toward him. "What's going on?"

"I got a call from Dr. Michaels over in Helena. He was brought in for a consult on a patient and while he was there was asked to basically rubber stamp a repeat prescription because another patient's doctor is out of town. Shane, being Shane, wouldn't just do that without seeing the patient, and he seems to have opened a can of worms. Twenty-one-year-old male diagnosed with schizophrenia."

"Well, I'm sorry to hear that, Brett, but what has that—" "He's definitely a shifter."

Asher wrinkled his nose. "That's impossible." Shifters never got human illnesses. Someone must have made a mistake. He knew Shane Michaels of course, human psychiatrist and really genuine guy, who also happened to be mated to a wolf shifter. He was one of the trusted human contacts who kept their eyes open for shifter kids in the system that might need a home.

It didn't happen often, thankfully, due to most shifters belonging to packs, but when it did it was a huge screw-up.

"I know, Asher, but Ginnie Michaels was with her husband and saw him briefly as well. Enough to know he's a shifter but not what exactly. You know what human hospitals are like. How it messes with your sense of smell."

"Exactly," Asher agreed, not sure what point Brett was trying to make. "And schizophrenia? That's what makes it impossible."

"Yeah, we know. But Ginnie says he's definitely a shifter. Apparently he's always been in care—no family—judged too unstable to be living in anything but a secure psychiatric facility." Brett paused, and Asher waited for him to say something else completely unbelievable. "Thing is, Asher, Ginnie's read the file that Shane got and she thinks he's a wolf omega."

Asher hauled out a laugh. Now he knew someone was pulling his leg. "Look, Brett—"

"If you don't believe me I suggest you face-time Ginnie Michaels, because Shane says she's been crying solidly for the past hour and demanding someone go get him."

That shut him up. "You're *serious*, aren't you."

"Like a heart attack."

"Do we know any history...at all?"

"No, only that the poor kid's been on anti-psychotic meds since he was twelve."

*How the hell?* Asher shook his head, clenching his fists. "I thought omegas were like pack royalty because they're so rare these days. How'd this happen?" Or female omegas, definitely. He'd never heard of a male omega. He didn't know such a thing even existed.

"What do you know about omegas, Asher?"

He groaned. This was turning into his most favorite conversation —*not*. "Is this multiple choice, Brett? 'Cause—"

"Okay, so I don't know much either, but Ginnie told me female omegas need to bond with an alpha male, usually their father, when they first start their menstrual cycle. Obviously, they're not claimed or mated, but they go seriously insane if not. Rages, like, off the charts."

"But this is a guy." Asher wasn't trying to be funny.

"And according to the history books, like, a thousand years ago omegas were always male. Female wolf omegas were never, ever heard of. Then all of a sudden it goes the other way and there hasn't been a male omega born in hundreds of years."

"What's he saying? Did he talk to him? Does he—"

"Asher, you know as much as I do. He's been shuffled around the system since he was a baby." Asher could hear the rustle of papers. "Hallucinations, both auditory and visual. Violent mood swings."

Asher wondered if a couple of his ex-girlfriends had been undiscovered omegas.

"This is serious, Asher."

*Fuck.* "You added reading minds to your resume?"

"I don't need it with you, but I bet Riley's laughing his ass off." Asher smiled. His brother Riley wasn't exactly a mind reader, but as a gifted healer and empath, he was as good as one.

"Deemed unsuitable for anything other than a locked psychiatric facility," Brett read out. "Shane was especially concerned about the level of medication he's been getting, and he's instructed it to be reduced."

Asher shook his head and then realized Brett couldn't see him. "Human drugs don't work the same on shifters. They would've had to have given him big doses." He glanced at his watch, realizing when he didn't get a reply he was stating the obvious. "You want me to go get him first thing tomorrow?"

"Actually, I want your ass out there now. Dr. Michaels kicked up a storm, and I think he's worried they may try to move him. Their new place is across state lines. Could be awkward."

"Do you have a name?

"Sai Daniels. Pronounced 'sigh,' spelled S-A-I."

"I'll be there in an hour." Asher grimly jotted down a few details and hung up.

His mom walked into the office, black hair swinging in her ubiquitous ponytail now streaked with gray that he and his brothers were no doubt responsible for. Brown eyes were surrounded by laugh lines. He hoped they were responsible for those as well.

"Emergency? Do you need us to stay?"

"Nah, Mom, we've got it covered. You go get ready." She hesitated, and he knew she was dying to ask. "I'm not even sure he's a shifter, Mom. I'll let you know," he fibbed smoothly, knowing the word omega or his age would be unusual enough to have his mom immediately canceling the cruise. Asher kissed her on the cheek. "Trust me," he scolded gently and smiled as he left the room. Their dad had surprised her with a monthlong cruise, and they were leaving that afternoon. First vacation on their own in nearly thirty years, and he and his brothers were all determined that nothing would spoil it. The three-year-old twin bear shifters they'd had for the last two years had just been successfully placed. Hunter's Creek only housed seven-year-old Jamie and fourteen-year-old Alex at the moment, and they could handle them.

Just then, the door opened and his brothers entered. Zack had to duck as he walked through. They were all huge. Both he and Riley were over six feet, but Zack was even bigger. Everyone always thought he and Riley were the twins, not Zack and Riley, which was funny because, strictly speaking, he wasn't related by blood to the two of them. He wasn't even the same shifter species, but he had been his mom and dad's first successful foster cub. Zack looked like their dad. He even had the same crooked nose, but Asher could see his mom in Riley. At thirty-three, they were older than him by four years.

"Zack, I need a ride."

Zack's eyebrows rose questioningly. "What's up, Asher, an emergency? Your latest date broke a nail?"

Asher ignored that. So he dated a lot, and yeah, they were usually high maintenance, but he had certain standards. Okay, so that was complete bull, but sometimes a reputation for being shallow was better than the real explanation. That subject was off limits even to them. "Yeah, Brett just called." He quickly gave them a rundown on their new arrival.

Riley interrupted. "How did Shane manage to get him released to us though? I mean, he's an adult, isn't he? Twenty-one's a bit old for a group home."

"I don't know." Asher shrugged. "To be honest, I don't care, so long as they did."

"Well, Cassie's finished college except for her exams, and Brett's obviously gonna be back soon. We don't have much going on except the Western Bank contract."

Asher nodded. His brothers ran a computer security firm. Riley was the computer geek behind the initial planning, and Zack, a licensed helicopter pilot, flew all over supervising installation work.

Riley looked at his twin. "I'll run Mom and Dad to the airport." Zack nodded. "Come on, then."

Asher checked all his IDs before following Zack out. He briefly fingered his FBI one and sighed. He had a feeling he was going to need it today. He only got asked to track missing people for them sometimes. He wasn't an actual agent, and he didn't do any *James Bond* shit, but whatever, it came in handy. Even if he just wanted to impress girlfriends with broken nails.

He paused a second and his heart gave the usual lurch, remembering smooth muscles, brown eyes, and the smell of Shiloh's football jersey from way back when before everything went to hell. *—or boyfriends.*

Asher stared out the window at the toy scenery below. His phone vibrated and he ignored the text from Sarah, who was getting their usual group together in town for the evening, and returned a call he had missed from Brett as they were setting off.

"Zack says we'll be at Billings Logan in about thirty minutes."
"Don't bother." Brett's voice was urgent. "Zack's cleared for a smaller private airfield a lot closer. He'll be getting instructions through right about now."

Zack was talking to someone via his headset, and the helicopter veered slightly.

"There'll be a car waiting. Shane has some pull, and if he didn't have an emergency patient himself to deal with, he'd be down there waiting for us."

The short silence that followed was deafening. Asher waited for more but nothing happened. "Brett, what aren't you telling me?"

Brett's sigh was troubled. "I've just been talking to Ginnie

Michaels again. The place is bad, Asher. Some hangover from the fifties. Mostly closed down, just a few elderly patients that are staying there. Anyone that needs locked supervision is going to their new place. No idea what our shifter's doing there, and I have no idea what state he's in. Ginnie only saw him by chance when she came in to bring Shane some files he needed. He doesn't think anyone has seen him for years. Think they were ready to throw away the key on this one."

"But *how*, Brett? This isn't the middle ages."

"Yeah, I know, but I think he's just slipped through the cracks. You know how overworked and underfunded the system is and when there's no family to complain, these patients get buried under all the paperwork and procedure. The nurses are doing a thankless job the best they can with little resources and lousy pay. I've seen this time and time again." He took a breath. "But not usually with a patient this young, I admit. I also wanted to warn you about the bitch in charge. Complete piece of work according to Ginnie. Says her husband has had a few run-ins with her over patient care. We're only giving them a few minutes' notice of your arrival and the transfer deliberately so they can't do anything."

"Christ, Brett, what the hell are they gonna do?" Asher asked, wondering if Brett wasn't being a bit too dramatic.

"Just giving you a heads up. Let me know when you land." "Anytime now."

"Okay, calling them now. Make sure you get to him pronto, Asher."

Asher hung up and looked at Zack as the blades slowed. "That was Brett. He's putting through our authorization now. He didn't want to give them prior warning, and apparently we've got to get to him quickly."

Zack nodded. "Asher, if I hadn't been there on some of the pick ups we've done, I wouldn't have believed what some sick people are capable of."

Asher knew, and he looked out the window as the helicopter

lowered down almost perfectly next to the black car waiting for them. He felt a twinge of guilt; Riley and Zack worked directly with the shifter council, a huge underground network of trusted humans and various shifters that kept their world and, more importantly, humans safe if a shifter went off the rails. It didn't happen often but when it did, it was serious. The last one had been a bear. He'd dropped his wife and son at the bank while he parked to fill out a mortgage application. An ordinary everyday occurrence, except the bank was robbed by a hopped-up psycho trying to get drug money. Three people had been fatally shot and two of them were his wife and child. In his grief he had shifted and run off after the guy. They were incredibly lucky CCTV hadn't caught him. They'd ended up with what the cops thought was a real bear on the loose until the emergency vet had been brought in—one of theirs— and managed to get him out of sight to shift back. It had been too damn close.

And up to now Asher hadn't really been involved in any of it. He'd grown up alongside shifters off every sort imaginable and for a lot of years hated every second of it. He'd just wanted to be normal. Hated the secrecy. Hated anything at school that would separate him from the rest of the kids. He'd often deliberately failed at sports when, as an eighth grader, he could have run rings around the senior star quarterback if he had wanted...which of course made him think about the other things he'd given up trying to be normal. He hadn't thought about that in months and now twice in the same day.

Asher relayed to Zack what Brett had told him.

Zack looked around the empty airfield. "Sorry, but I can't just leave it here. I'm going to have to wait until you get back."

Asher nodded, wishing he had thought to bring his sister Cassie, who was a student nurse, with him. But he shrugged. *Okay then.* After flashing his ID a few times at various gates, he found himself shown into a small office. The mousy guy who'd told him to wait hadn't impressed Asher one bit. He smelled of stale cigarettes and beer, and the surroundings were creeping the shit out of him. Hell, the place looked like it should have been shut down a hundred years ago. Peeling, stained walls and floors weren't agreeing with his shifter sense of smell at all. Disinfectant, he expected, and that would have been bad enough, but the place took Hitchcock to a whole other level. He half-expected a film crew to walk by.

A thin, fiftyish woman walked into the office. "Mr. Hunter?" she asked, looking at the papers in her hand and not bothering to introduce herself. "This is most irregular. We've only just received the transfer orders for Mr. Daniels, and he isn't ready. It would be better if you made an appointment for tomorrow."

"No, I'm sorry. I have my transport waiting. I'm afraid we have to go immediately."

"Well, that's really problematic." The woman flushed, frowning. Asher could smell the unease grow in her and wondered if Brett hadn't been exaggerating how quickly they needed to get Sai after all. "I'm sorry, but I will have to make some phone calls to verify these orders. Mr. Daniels was due to be transferred today to our new facility." A brittle smile striving for sympathy cracked her heavily made-up face. "He's a real desperate case, and we feel he needs a higher degree of monitoring."

Just as Asher opened his mouth to demand he be taken to Mr. Daniel's room immediately, a terrified cry rent the air and every hair on the back of his neck stood up. Cursing himself for not taking Brett's warning seriously enough, he took off in the direction of the noise.

Heart hammering, his nostrils flared. More powerful than the stench of unwashed bodies and moldy furnishings, he smelled bleach, panic, and worst of all, fear.

Charging through a door, he processed the god-awful scene in two seconds. Two big, burly guys, looking more at home in a concentration camp than a hospital, were struggling to hold a smaller man down on the bed—ridiculous given their size. A woman, either a nurse or a doctor holding a syringe, was fighting with the man trying to avoid the needle. Asher's nose barely registered the nurse as some type of shifter a few seconds before he also processed the patient as one and knew this was whom he had come to collect.

Asher roared in fury. With one powerful swipe, he leveled both guys, and in another second he had a hold on the woman's arm, stopping her from dispensing the shot. Sai scrambled off the bed and curled up in the corner of the room.

"How dare you!" spluttered the gray-haired woman as Asher forcibly curved the needle at a ninety-degree angle and dropped it onto the tray.

Asher didn't give her time to continue. "This patient is for immediate transport. Dr. Michaels was clear he was to have no more drugs. If you doubt those instructions, I can get Dr. Michaels on the phone." Asher glared and released her arm. "Lady—and I use that term generously—I can get the fucking FBI on the phone. Now get the hell *out.*" The woman glared at him but ran out the door.

Asher breathed a huge sigh. God, he hadn't been that close to losing his temper for many years, especially around humans. As kids, they'd always been brought up to respect their shifter strength, and no human—as big as those two guys were—could go up against all five hundred pounds of Asher's animal when he was in full shift. *Not all humans though,* as he remembered the smell of the nurse with the syringe. He instantly dismissed the thought as he realized he had more important worries.

Asher hunkered down in front of the shaking form curled up in the corner. *Humanity?* Some people didn't know the meaning of the word.

Asher hesitated as he took him in. The faint smell of shifter was there but the stench of the place made it difficult to categorize, and he wished again he had his mom or Cassie with him. He also acknowledged that Brett had it right. They were drugging him for transport, and he'd gotten there just in time.

His eyes fastened on the trembling figure in front of him. Short gasps tore out of the man's throat. Head hunched down, arms tightened around knees clasped against his chest as if he were hanging on. Filthy sweats, worse than some he'd thrown away. Goosebumps pricking his bare arms. The only bright thing in his muddy looking, matted hair, was red. A drop. God, had they hit him? He hid his face, alternating between shivering and rocking. He looked cold. *What the hell did they do to you?*

Asher cleared his throat. He had to get him out of there and didn't have time to be gentle.

"Sai? We need to move you."

He placed one hand on Sai's shaking forearm and caught the swift arc of his arm trying to connect with his face. *Whoa. Well, that was definitely a reaction. Taking me on?* He'd have laughed if it were funny—at all.

"No one's gonna hurt you. Don't you wanna get out of here? Mmm? There ya go." Asher shrugged out of his own sweatshirt and calmly widened the neck so it would slide over him easily.

Thin arms stiffened but stayed still, and Sai's chest rose at a slower rate when Asher gently pulled the sweatshirt past his eyes. "So you're not ready to try and take me out, huh?"

Sai lifted his face finally and pure amber eyes, *wolf* eyes, stared into his own. Asher rocked back on his heels as a sheer sense of want gripped his chest almost painfully and rippled out into tendrils of deep belonging as his tiger claimed the wolf as his own.

*Oh God, now? Here?*

Of all times and in all places, stuck in some dingy shit excuse for a hospital, with some man—*boy?*—who looked like he needed far more care than Asher could give, it had happened. His cat clawed frantically at him to get out, nearly bowling him over in the rush to get to Sai.

*Mate.*

Asher growled and hung his head in despair. He hadn't been able to smell Sai properly because of everything else, and it had taken brushing the side of his arm as he lifted his face for him to know. God, what a mess.

*Mate.*

A soft touch pulled his gaze. Possessiveness whirled around Asher as he struggled not to gather his mate up and bury him in his arms. Need stabbed him. Confusion chased the gold flecks in his gorgeous eyes, and Asher wanted it gone. He wanted those incredible eyes clear and focused...*on me.*

Asher knew deep down Sai would feel the connection, but his ignorance and whatever drugs he had in his system masked it. Sai lifted a shaky hand to touch the side of Asher's face in obvious bewilderment but still didn't say one word. Deep purple marks marred Sai's neck. Asher's chest tightened and a shallow breath managed to escape his lungs. He took in his pale face under the bruises and gazed at the chipped stubs of filthy, bitten fingernails as Sai lowered his hand back to his side. As if worn out. No, as if he had expected too much and given up.

Asher pulled himself together. "Sai, we need to get you out of here, okay?" He tried to encourage him to stand and after a few seconds, Sai managed to on shaky legs. He was tall—about a head smaller than him—but his body was so thin, so *wasted,* for the first time in many years Asher wanted to cry at the injustice of people—humans or shifters—that would treat another life, another *soul,* like this.

He took one look around the bare room and didn't bother to ask Sai if he needed to take anything. Taking one cautious step, Sai tried to walk, but his knees buckled. Asher caught him easily. Without thinking, he brushed a kiss to his mate's forehead and looked into those big eyes fighting to stay open. Sai blinked at him slowly, easier breaths ghosting his face, and Asher's heart hammered as Sai's head lowered to rest against his chest.

*Yes.*

In that small, cautious, trusting movement, Asher heard his

animal roar protectively as he tightened his arms around Sai. No one would ever hurt a hair on his head again. While Asher still had breath left in his body, Sai would be safe, he would be cared for, and he would be *loved*.

Read more about Sai and Asher HERE

# About Victoria Sue

Victoria Sue fell in love with love stories as a child when she would hide away with her mom's library books and dream of the dashing hero coming to rescue her from math homework. She never mastered math but never stopped loving her heroes and decided to give them the happy ever afters they fight so hard for.

She loves reading and writing about gorgeous boys loving each other the best—and creating a family for them to adore. Thrilled to hear from her readers, she can be found most days lurking on Facebook where she doesn't need factor 1000 sun-cream to hide her freckles.

www.victoriasue.com

For the latest news, deals, stories and more, sign up for Victoria Sue's Newsletter.

Join Victoria Sue's Crew (Facebook reader group) to discuss all things Victoria Sue, participate in member only contests, and more!

facebook.com/sue.kellett
instagram.com/victoriasueauthor
amazon.com/Victoria-Sue/e/B00OSTTZ0K
bookbub.com/author/victoris-sue

# Also by Victoria Sue

**Love MPreg?**

Check out these series and single title by Victoria Sue.

**Standalone Novels**

Daddy's Girl*

*An Alpha who hates omegas. An omega who hates Alphas. Forced together by circumstances, both men are determined to see their arrangement through. Except the longer they stay together, neither of them is sure they want it to end.*

**Series**

Sirius Wolves*

*According to legend, when humankind is at its most desperate, the goddess Sirius will send three of the most powerful werewolf shifters ever created to save mankind. The alphas, Blaze, Conner and Darric, find their omega in Aden. They become true mates, fulfilling the ancient prophecy and forming Orion's Circle. Now, the battle against terrorist group The Winter Circle has begun.*

Shifter Rescue*

*911 for vulnerable shifters when there's no where else for them to run.*

Unexpected Daddies

*Daddy kink with heart and heat. No ABDL.*

Heroes and Babies

*Protective men find love while fighting to save a child. Contemporary suspense with heart-pounding action.*

Guardians of Camelot

*Hundreds of years ago, facing defeat, the witch Morgana sent monsters into* the future to vanquish a humanity King Arthur wouldn't be able to save. The King might have won the battle, but now, centuries later, a few chosen men will have to fight the war. To battle an ancient evil, the greatest weapon each hero will have is each other.

## Enhanced World

This series follows an enhanced H.E.R.O. team to provide the right mix of action and romance. This series is the perfect for fans of romance with a blend of military/law enforcement, urban fantasy and superheroes. As one reviewer put it, "This story was like S.W.A.T. meets X-men meets The Fantastic Four."

## His First*

Omegaverse at it's finest! Set in the future, these novels pack in all the feels, while still wrapping up with a wonderfully sweet ending. Whether you've never tried MPREG or you're just looking for your next favorite Alpha/Omega pairing, check out the His First series.

## Rainbow Key

Rainbow Key is an idyllic island retreat off the west coast of Florida. Think wedding destination, white sandy beaches, lurve... except at the moment Joshua is struggling to pay the electricity bill, they've no paying customers, and even if they did they can't afford the repairs from the devastating hurricane that struck three years ago. Then there's Matt who just got let out of prison, Charlie who ran away from home, and Ben, a famous model until a devastating house fire destroyed his face. Welcome to Rainbow Key — held together by love, family, and sticky tape.

## Kingdom of Askara*

The Kingdom of Askara has been torn apart by conflict for centuries, where humans exist as subservient beings to their werewolf masters. Legend says it will only be able to heal itself when an Alpha King and a pure omega are mated and crowned together, but a pure omega hasn't been born in over a thousand years.

## Innocents

A captivating historical duology set in Regency London. The Innocent Auction: It started with a plea for help and ended with forbidden love, the love between a Viscount and a stable-boy. An impossible love and a guarantee of the hangman's noose. The Innocent Betrayal: Two broken souls. One so damaged he thinks he doesn't deserve love, and one so convinced he would never find it he has stopped looking. Danger, lies, and espionage. The fate of hundreds of English soldier's lives depending on them to trust each other, to work together.

## Pure

A madman has been kidnapping, torturing and murdering submissives. Join Callum, Joe and Damon as they race against the clock to stop the killings, while they each find love with a submissive. This trilogy of romantic thrillers is set against the backdrop of BDSM club Pure.

## Hunter's Creek*

The Hunter's Creek novels will draw you in with action and keep you hooked until each satisfying HEA. This series won't disappoint fans of shifters, fated mates or MPREG.

*Stories contain MPREG

Made in the USA
Middletown, DE
06 August 2023